BANANA SPLIT PERSONALITIES

CRIME À LA MODE, BOOK 4

CHRISTY BARRITT

CHAPTER ONE

"BANANA SPLITS!" Serena Lavinia yelled. "Get one before your kids throw fits!"

People of all ages flocked around Serena's ice cream truck, appropriately named Elsa. It was the first annual Beach, Books, and Banana Splits Children's Festival here on Lantern Beach, and the town had gone all out for the event.

Actors dressed as storybook characters strolled around the boardwalk. A woman strumming a ukulele played rollicking songs under a nearby gazebo. There were craft stations, scavenger hunts, and even some type of dance party taking place on a temporary stage across the sand dunes.

Based on how many banana splits she'd sold,

Serena would say this event was a rousing success.

The event coordinator had personally invited Serena to sell her ice cream, especially since the sweet treats fit the theme of the festival. Serena had jumped in with both feet and had even dressed up like an ice cream cone. Her shirt looked like scoops of strawberry and mint, she'd found a brown skirt and added a waffle print design to it, and she'd made a headband that looked like an upside down ice cream cone had melted on her hair.

The kids had *loved* it.

Maybe she'd found her place in life—around children who appreciated her playful costumes, odd sales pitches, and quirky ice cream truck.

Serena's muscles tightened when she spotted a large group of kids heading her way. Whenever the line got long, things began to feel chaotic. Her operation wasn't a large one, and she wasn't used to dealing with such high demand.

She glanced back at her temporary coworker, Webster Newsom, and warned him. "Brace yourself. We've got a crowd coming from the 'Pirate of the Caribbean' show. In my experience, pirates are always hangry . . . arr than most."

"Consider me braced." He held up a canister of whipped cream, his finger poised on the trigger. "And good job talking pirate-ese."

Serena had known she would need an extra hand for this event. When her friend and newspaper editor had volunteered to help, she hadn't refused.

Her dog, Scoops, barked at her feet, as if letting Serena know he was at her service also.

"I promise to reward you with an orange push-up pop if you behave," she murmured.

The little terrier barked again and wagged his tail as if he understood.

As a line formed, Serena began taking orders.

But one little boy in particular kept eyeballing her, his scrutiny unavoidable. He was probably ten, about twenty pounds overweight, and he hadn't yet grown into his teeth. He obviously had something he wanted to say based on his laser-like stare.

"I'm hungry," he groused after he'd placed his order. "Can you work faster?"

"I'm doing my best." Serena put on her most cheerful voice.

"But I'm hot. I want my banana split, and I want it now!"

Serena tried not to scowl. She was working on her customer service skills—she'd even been watching YouTube videos on the subject. But this boy seemed to be testing every last principle she'd been trying to put into practice.

Maybe she hadn't found her people here after all.

"Skippy." A woman with a stern voice rushed up to him, appearing slightly out of breath. "You need to step back and think about your words. I simply will not tolerate you talking to adults like this. Do you understand?"

Based on the woman's tone, this had to be the boy's mom. Serena was grateful someone had set him straight. He'd been downright rude.

With a scowl and a kick to the sidewalk, Skippy stomped toward the other side of her ice cream truck.

Once he was gone, the woman turned to Serena, tucking one of many wayward brown hairs behind her ear. She looked hot, frazzled, and tired—not like a mom who was having fun and posting family photos online that people would envy.

If her son acted like that all day, Serena could

understand why the woman looked as bedraggled as she did.

"I'm so sorry about that." A frown consumed the woman's face. "It seems like I realized a little bit too late the effects of spoiling your child. Now I'm trying to break him of feeling entitled, and it's so painful that I want to bury my head in the sand."

"You don't want to do that." Serena added some whip cream atop a banana split. "It's hard to breathe under there. I tried it once."

The woman stared at her, as if trying to figure out if Serena was joking or not.

Serena decided that she would keep her in suspense, just for fun.

As Serena handed the woman the banana split, Skippy appeared again. It was like the boy had picked up on the scent of ice cream like a wolf smelling fear.

But, instead of grabbing his treat, the boy stared up at Serena, his eyes narrowed with scrutiny. "Why is there blood on the front of your truck?"

"There's no blood on the front of my truck." A chuckle trailed Serena's statement. Why in the world would the boy say something absurd like that?

"Yes, there is. I saw it. I touched it." He held up his hand, displaying a red liquid that stained his fingertips.

Serena narrowed her eyes as she stared at his hand. Her throat tightened at the picture it formed.

"It was probably just some berries. There's a mulberry tree near where I park." Even as Serena said the words, she knew good and well that mulberries would leave a pinkish-purple stain—not brownish red.

"It's not berries."

"Then maybe some kids spilled strawberry sauce on the truck." Serena gritted her teeth while still trying to smile. It took every ounce of her energy to do so. "I do put that on my banana splits."

"It's not strawberry sauce. Do you want me to taste it?" Skippy brought his finger to his mouth in slow motion, as if trying to add more drama to the moment.

"No!" Horror washed through Serena. "Please, don't put your finger in your mouth. In fact, wash your hands. I'll check it out. Would that make you happy?"

The boy smiled, looking a little too satisfied at getting the response he wanted.

Based on Skippy's actions, Serena wouldn't be surprised if the boy had planted something on her truck's grill just to get attention or cause a ruckus.

Serena climbed from Elsa and tried not to stomp as she circled the edge of her vehicle. This seemed like a royal waste of time, and she had a whole line of customers waiting to be served— that also meant she had money to be made. Money that would help pay her bills.

She fully expected to see some ketchup. Maybe Kool-Aid. Or that strawberry sauce was still a possibility.

But as Serena examined Elsa's hood, she sucked in a breath.

Something brownish red *was* splattered all over the front. Some of the liquid had even pooled in the crevices of the lattice-like grill and wasn't yet dry. The combination of high humidity and shade from the canopy at the booth beside Serena had most likely kept the liquid tacky in a few areas.

As much as Serena wanted to believe that some type of edible liquid had been spewed there, her gut told her that wasn't the case. The effect looked downright criminal.

Webster appeared beside her, holding Scoops in his arms. He pushed his glasses up higher on his nose. In this heat and humidity, the plastic frames didn't want to stay in place. "Is everything okay?"

Serena shook her head, trying to push down the nausea that wanted to form. "No, I'm afraid everything isn't okay. I'm going to need to call Chief Chambers. Now."

———

POLICE CHIEF CASSIDY CHAMBERS held a camera in her hands and frowned as she studied the front of Serena's truck. "So a kid noticed this?"

"That's right," Serena confirmed.

She stood beside Cassidy with Scoops in her arms—Webster had handed the dog off to her. Unobstructed sunlight showered them from directly overhead. Sweat trickled down Serena's spine and across her forehead, but she tried not to complain. Besides, she had bigger worries.

"I don't make it a habit of examining the outside of my truck every morning," Serena continued. "Perhaps I need to add that to my list."

"Perhaps you do." Cassidy took another picture, her voice giving no indication as to what she was thinking. Instead, the police chief bent lower to get a different angle on the spatter.

Her blonde hair was pulled into a tight bun at the nape of her neck, and her tanned skin gave her a healthy glow. Most people, when they first met Cassidy, didn't guess she led the town's police department. But, despite her youthful, pretty appearance, she was as tough as nails and had led this town like a pro through some pretty serious crises.

Serena clenched her teeth and frowned, uneasy with this development. "Are you sure this is blood?"

Scoops barked in her arms, as if he echoed her concerns.

"That's what the test said." Cassidy held up a plastic bag with a swab she'd taken. She'd dripped some kind of chemical on the cotton tip and had watched as it turned pink. "And the test doesn't lie. However, what we don't know for sure is if the blood is from a human or an animal."

Serena held Scoops closer. "They both sound bad."

"The good news is that there's no dent in the front of your truck. There are no indications of a hit-and-run."

"Of course not. I would never do that." Serena didn't bother to restrain the outrage from her voice. Did Cassidy really think she'd do that?

"But if that's the case…" Cassidy tapped her pen against her lips as she paused. "…then that means a crime may have occurred within the vicinity of your truck. Where do you usually park Elsa?"

"At my camper. It was there yesterday evening until about eight o'clock."

"Were you nearby the whole evening?"

"No. I went on a walk at the beach with Scoops and . . ." Serena cleared her throat, not wanting to start any rumors on the small island. ". . . Webster. When we got back, Webster went with me to drop the truck off at the boardwalk in preparation for the festival today."

Cassidy turned and examined the area

around them. "I don't see anything suspicious on the surrounding booths. So it appears that, if something did happen, it probably occurred at your place."

"If something happened while I was home, I would've noticed," Serena assured.

Cassidy gave her a knowing look. "Not if you were taking a walk on the beach."

Serena wanted to argue, but she knew she couldn't. Cassidy's explanation was perfectly plausible. The window of time was large enough that a crime could have occurred while she was gone.

"So what now?" Serena stared at Elsa, feeling like her truck was a wayward child needing discipline. Or maybe a wayward child that needed a hug after trauma.

Serena wasn't sure which. As if on cue, Elsa began playing, "The Battle Hymn of the Republic."

"Your timing is uncanny," Serena muttered.

She should be used to her truck randomly playing songs at the most inoperative times . . .

Even Cassidy gave the truck a dirty look before leveling her gaze. "I need to go back to your place and examine things there. I need to locate the area where this crime occurred."

"Maybe there is no crime scene," Serena reminded her. "Maybe somebody cut themselves and had a . . . projectile blood spurt?"

Cassidy stared at her, needing no words to convey her thoughts. She was clearly not on the same page as Serena. Deep inside, Serena knew her theory was outlandish but . . . she hated any other alternative.

"What if it was a prank? I mean, not everyone has evil intentions." Serena was trying to convince herself just as much as she was trying to convince Cassidy.

"You're right. But until I know that for sure, I need to treat this as a criminal investigation. I'm going to need you to shut Elsa down and leave her here until we know what's going on. Officer Leggott is going to guard the scene—while hopefully reassuring the children and parents at the festival that there's nothing to be concerned about. You and I are going to go back to your place so we can check it out."

Serena could read between the lines. Cassidy didn't want Serena going back by herself. They needed to go together, just in case Serena decided to cover up any evidence.

Unfortunately, Serena had been through this so many times that she halfway felt like a police officer herself.

"Okay," Serena said. "Let's go. Can I take Scoops in the car with me?"

"Sure thing." Cassidy motioned to Officer Leggott to take his place near Elsa before waving her hand to let Serena know she should follow.

Serena quickly asked Webster to remain with Elsa while she was gone. Knowing Webster, he was already mentally writing an article on this.

Then Cassidy and Serena walked to the police SUV and climbed inside.

As for Serena . . . she was just glad to have Webster here to lend a hand. He'd already been a real lifesaver more than once, and his friendship was proving to be invaluable.

CHAPTER TWO

AN HOUR LATER, Cassidy had examined the camper Serena called home. She'd talked to neighbors, none of whom had seen anything the night before. She'd also called in some additional officers to check the surrounding areas for a sign of anything suspicious.

So far, it looked like all Cassidy's hard work was for nothing.

Just as Serena had suspected.

Serena wasn't sure where that blood on Elsa had come from, but it was obviously a joke. Maybe somebody had been grilling out and raw meat juice had been flung in this direction.

Would that register as blood? And was raw meat juice even the correct terminology?

Serena wasn't sure. But certainly, there must be a good explanation for today's turn of events.

As Serena watched the officers work, she stood on the edge of her property. She leased a little plot at a local campground. Many locals stayed here since real estate prices on the island were high due to the overwhelming number of vacation homes.

But Serena loved living here. Her little camper with the turquoise stripe across the front felt like home. She even had a deck out front with a hammock nestled in the corner.

Some people might think that living here was beneath them. But, to Serena, those people were the ones missing out. The simple life was a great life.

Finally, the police chief walked back toward her, a slight frown playing across her lips. "We didn't find anything, Serena. I'm not sure what's going on, and I'm not closing the book on this investigation yet. But you're in the clear. For now."

Serena gave her a look, not bothering to hide that she felt insulted. "After everything we've been through, you *still* think I might be guilty?"

The two of them had been thrown into quite a few adventures together in the two years they'd known each other. This summer had been one for the books. Thankfully, Serena had experienced several nice, uneventful weeks here of late.

No dead bodies. No crimes. Just happy, lazy days filled with selling ice cream on this little island.

"You know I'm just doing my job," Cassidy reminded her.

"I know. And your thoroughness is one reason why you're so good at it." Serena meant the words. Cassidy was a kind of role model for Serena—though Cassidy didn't know that.

"Thank you." Cassidy slid her phone, where she'd been taking notes, back into her pocket. "We've looked Elsa over and didn't find anything else on her. You're free to bring her home. But if you see anything suspicious, I expect you to let me know."

"Of course." Who did Cassidy think Serena was? An amateur or something? Never.

Except sometimes, she was. Most of the time, for that matter.

"I'll give you a ride back to the children's

festival," Cassidy continued. "For now, let's try to keep this development quiet. I don't want to scare all the kids away. As far as they know, this could just be juice from a maraschino cherry off one of your banana splits."

"Got it." Another thought jarred Serena. "Although Webster may not want to keep this quiet . . . the news on the island lately has been rather ho-hum."

Webster *was* the editor of the island's newspaper as well as a gung ho reporter. Stuff like this was what articles were made of, especially in a relatively sleepy town like Lantern Beach.

Cassidy gave her a look. "You don't think you can convince him to keep quiet?"

"Have you met the man?" Serena's voice rose an octave. "He's pretty determined."

Besides, if Serena wasn't directly involved in this, she'd be jumping all over the opportunity to cover a story like this. Being a journalist was in her DNA, even if the career was just part-time.

"I wouldn't want to see you get the bad press . . ." Cassidy gave her a knowing look.

"Point taken." News like this could hurt Serena's business.

She and Webster had each other's backs . . .

right? At least, that's how it had seemed in the past.

"If there's no crime, I'm not really sure what there is to report about," Serena said with a nod.

"Exactly."

Now she had to make sure Webster was on the same page.

"Okay, come on." Cassidy motioned for Serena to follow. "Let's get you and Scoops back to the festival. Ty is fixing me crab cakes back at the house, and my mouth has been watering for them all day."

"I would hate to stand between you and your crab cakes." Serena climbed back into Cassidy's SUV and placed Scoops in her lap.

But Serena's mind was far from banana splits or crab cakes.

All she could think about was that blood spatter on the front of Elsa.

What had her truck gotten itself into?

SERENA SAT with Webster inside her ice cream truck, which had officially closed down for the rest of the day. Since the festival had wound down, that was fine by her.

All the windows to the truck were closed so no one could see or hear them. But the AC ran, preventing the space from feeling like an oven inside.

"So it really was blood?" Webster repeated, taking a sip of his chocolate milkshake.

The treat was one of the perks of working for Serena—free ice cream.

He leaned back against a freezer, his legs stretched out in front of him. Serena sat across from him, settling for a cold bottle of water instead. And Scoops . . . the dog had curled up in the corner, finally deciding to take a nap after today's excitement.

"That's right," Serena said. "It was blood. Can you believe it?"

Webster shook his head, not trying to hide his surprise. "How do these things always happen to you, Serena?"

"I ask myself that quite often. I'm not sure." She seemed to be a crime magnet lately.

She stared at Webster for a moment.

Things had been different between the two of them over the past few weeks. They were still in friendship territory. But Serena felt like something had shifted between them, and she wasn't sure what.

It shouldn't matter. Webster wasn't her type.

He was good-looking in a smart, nerdy kind of way. But she'd always seen herself with someone who was her opposite, who was more of the athletic type.

The athletic type? For some reason, the thought suddenly caught her off guard.

Would Serena ever really be happy with someone who liked to work out all the time in order to keep up his physique? Someone who might even dare ask her to go hiking or surfing or do CrossFit?

That sounded horrible.

She certainly wasn't fit, and she despised working out. But opposites attracted, right? Maybe she needed someone like that to balance her out, to be the yin to her yang.

Or . . . maybe what Serena thought she wanted really wasn't what she wanted, and what she needed was really not at all what she'd envisioned. Romance was so confusing, so she tried not to think about the subject.

She preferred to stick her head in the sand,

as the saying went. Figuratively, not literally. Unlike what Skippy's mom might think.

"So what now?" Webster stared at her, waiting for her response.

"Now, Cassidy said I could take Elsa home. She wants me to keep this quiet, for the kids' sake."

"Can't blame her for that."

"No, I can't either." Relief washed through Serena. Webster didn't appear to want to jump on this for an article. That was a good thing. "I don't know what to think about this. I'm just going to have to assume the blood was an accident or a joke. There are no police reports indicating anyone's been hurt. None of my neighbors saw anything either."

"Most of your neighbors are either at the beach surfing or they're high. You and I both know that's the truth." He gave her a knowing look.

Serena frowned, wanting to refute his words and defend her neighbors. "*Most* is an overstatement. Some very nice—and responsible— people live at the campground."

Webster wasn't all wrong, however. Part of the beach-bum lifestyle did involve surfing, drinking, and a good deal of drugs. Not for everyone. But for a lot of people.

And surfers loved living at the campground since prices were so cheap.

"I'm not saying they're not nice," Webster continued. "But I am saying that it's a gathering place for hippies. They're not really known for being the most observant, especially not if there are good waves to catch."

Webster was finally starting to catch onto island life. A good day of surfing was always followed by a good night of partying.

Serena let out a sigh before taking another sip of her water. "This whole thing just seems crazy to me."

"As it would with anyone."

She stood, the ceiling just tall enough for her to stretch to her five-foot-three height in her truck. She quickly looked at her inventory and paused.

"What's wrong?" Webster asked.

"I should have more ice cream sandwiches. I just restocked them. Did you sell any while I was gone?"

"Maybe one."

She grunted. "Weird."

Her inventory was the least of her problems right now. Maybe she'd miscounted—but she didn't think so. Serena would have to figure it out later.

"I guess I should get home," Serena said. "I've got that article on the latest beach art to work on."

"I guess you should." Webster stood, stooping down as he turned toward her. "I'll follow you."

"Why would you follow me?"

"I'd feel better knowing you got home safely. At least until we have some answers about what's going on."

Serena shrugged, realizing there would be no harm in Webster doing so. "Fine. Have it your way. I just hate for you to waste your time."

"Anything with you is never a waste of time." Webster offered a quick smile before pushing his glasses higher up on his nose. As if he realized what he'd said, he pointed over his shoulder behind him. "I'm going to go get my car. I'll meet you out by the exit of the parking lot. Sound good?"

"Sounds great. I'll see you there."

Serena had to admit that he looked kind of cute when he acted awkward like that.

Webster? Cute?

Serena felt like she was getting as soft as her ice cream—after she left her truck unplugged on a ninety-degree day.

CHAPTER THREE

AS SERENA WATCHED Webster walk toward his car, she lifted Scoops and stepped outside in the mid-August heat. She wanted to look at the front of her truck again.

It was silly. She knew it was.

But she felt like she had a bond with this truck.

She and Elsa were both a little different. A little quirky. They liked to march to the beat of their own drummers, as the saying went. And they were both a staple around town, their colorful antics giving people something to talk about.

Serena patted the hood and stared at the

little reddish-brown blotches that still remained. Despite the heat, she shivered.

"What happened, girl?" she whispered. "Those cops were all up in your grill. Literally."

Serena halfway expected Elsa to answer or to start randomly playing a song.

She knew the songs that arbitrarily rang out from her truck were because of a mechanical glitch. Serena also knew the glitch would cost more to fix than she wanted to spend. Besides, Serena kind of liked not knowing what song was going to come out of Elsa at any time.

"You didn't do anything naughty, did you?" she continued.

Of course, Elsa didn't respond.

"Do you always talk to your truck?" someone said.

Serena swirled around and saw the little boy from earlier. The one who discovered the blood. Skippy.

She instantly tensed.

"Who says I'm not talking to my dog?" Serena held Scoops close to her.

The boy narrowed his eyes and smirked. "You look like you're talking to your truck. Did you get the *strawberry sauce* cleaned off?"

The way he said strawberry sauce made it clear he didn't believe that's what he'd found earlier.

"I'm going to do that as soon as I get home, if you must know." Serena glanced around. "Where's your mom?"

"She's a slow walker. She'll be here soon. She's making me go to some type of stupid sing-along." He crossed his arms and pouted.

"I'm sure it will be fun." Serena felt sorry for whoever was leading that session. They would definitely have their hands full with Skippy there.

"Yeah, just as much fun as eating a banana split with slivered liver on top. Have a great evening."

Before Serena could say anything else, Skippy scrambled down the boardwalk. She looked in the distance and spotted the boy's mom running after him, calling his name. But he didn't slow down.

Serena's heart went out to that woman.

She didn't have time to think about Skippy any more now. Webster was waiting for her.

She climbed in Elsa and pulled away from the boardwalk into the parking lot. Webster waited ahead near the exit. He motioned to her, and Serena pulled in front of him and onto the highway.

No doubt, she'd be thinking about this turn of events all night. Maybe all week. But that blood spatter was probably nothing, she tried to reassure herself. There had to be a perfectly logical explanation for it.

But if it was nothing, why did Serena have to keep reminding herself of that fact?

She frowned.

Several minutes later, Lantern Beach's retail area disappeared from her rearview mirror as Serena headed back toward her place.

As Serena neared her turn at the entrance to the campground, she eased off the gas and pressed on the brakes.

Nothing happened.

She sucked in a breath as the first wave of panic washed through her.

She couldn't make the turn without slowing down first. The truck would tip if she tried that going this speed.

She pressed on the brakes harder.

Still nothing.

"Elsa . . . what's going on?" Serena's hands

gripped the steering wheel so tightly that her fingers began to ache.

Just then, Elsa began to play "The Wheels on the Bus."

Serena muttered under her breath at the vehicle. It was almost like Elsa was telling her that those very wheels were going to keep going round and round, whether Serena liked it or not.

And Serena most definitely *didn't* like it.

She needed to slow the vehicle. Pedestrians walked the edges of this street. In the opposite direction, cars sped toward their destinations on the two-lane highway. Even though Serena could still control the steering wheel, she needed to control her speed also.

Just beyond the entrance to her campground, a stretch of woods came into view. Serena continued to press on the brakes, throwing her weight onto the pedal.

Her efforts were futile.

Behind her, Webster pressed on his horn, almost as if he knew something was wrong.

Another wave of panic surged inside her.

How was she going to get out of this in one piece?

Ahead, some pedestrians started across the

road. She hit the brakes again, desperate to slow down and gain control of the vehicle.

But she couldn't. Elsa wouldn't let her.

Instead, Serena jerked the wheel to the right, trying to avoid the family of five who were loaded down with beach gear and oblivious to her runaway truck.

She narrowly missed them.

But she *had* missed them.

Her relief was short-lived.

Instead, she found herself careening toward a tree.

"Scoops—hold on!"

She prayed that they would walk away from this incident unscathed.

But it wasn't looking good.

CHAPTER FOUR

ELSA STOPPED mere inches before slamming into the tree and the engine shut off.

Serena dragged in shallow breaths as she stared at the oak directly in front of her. Her life had flashed before her eyes. Her heart still pounded out of control.

That had been too close.

"Are you okay, Scoops?" She glanced down at the dog who sat on the floor beside her.

Her canine wagged his tail, acting like he'd enjoyed the adrenaline rush as much as he enjoyed a good squirrel chase.

She rubbed his head, grateful they were both unharmed.

But what had happened?

She looked down at Elsa's dashboard and scowled. "Thanks a lot."

As she said the words, the music outside died. That was right. The wheels on this bus were no longer going round and round.

Webster appeared at her window, his eyes orbs of concern as he stared inside at her. "Serena, are you okay?"

She lifted Scoops into her arms as she opened her door. "We're fine."

Webster stepped back and let out an exasperated breath. He'd really been worried. He'd had good reason. Things could have turned out a lot differently.

"What happened?" he asked, helping her onto the grass.

"I don't know." As Serena put her weight on both legs, she felt her knees buckle. She was more shaken than she'd realized. "The brakes just wouldn't work."

"That's weird." Webster pushed his glasses higher again.

"I know. I've never had this problem before— and I've had a lot of problems with this ice cream truck."

"At least no one was hurt." Webster glanced

behind him at the family who'd been crossing the road when the accident occurred. They stood on the other side of the road, giving Serena dirty looks, almost as if she'd tried to plow them down on purpose.

Serena briefly considered giving them ice cream as her way of saying sorry. But her limbs were shaking so badly that she didn't think she could. She needed to gather herself for another moment.

Webster turned back to her. "Will the truck start?"

When the vehicle had come to the sudden stop, the motor had seemed to die. It was weird, but Serena wasn't complaining. She would have hit that tree otherwise.

"Let me see."

She handed Scoops to Webster and climbed back inside, secretly grateful to sit down. She tried to crank the engine, but nothing happened. She tried again with the same results. Finally, she shrugged.

"It looks like I need to call the tow truck," Serena said.

"Here, let me try."

The two switched places. Serena held Scoops

now and let Webster do his man thing, which was basically the same thing she'd just done, only done by a man.

He tried to start the engine, but nothing happened for him either.

Just as Serena had figured. She didn't say that, though.

Webster finally shrugged as he turned toward her. "I guess you're right. We should probably call the tow truck. I can give you a ride home in the meantime."

Serena glanced around. Cars had begun to pass behind her. She was far enough off the road that they could safely do that.

But, considering everything that had happened, she didn't feel safe leaving her truck here.

"I think I'll wait here with Elsa," she finally said. "I'd feel better keeping my eyes on her."

"Whatever you're comfortable with. Do you want me to call the truck for you?"

Webster was so thoughtful like that sometimes.

Serena nodded. "I'd really appreciate that."

"Of course. That's what friends are for." But

as he said the words, his cheeks turned a subtle shade of pink.

What about saying that had embarrassed him?

Serena didn't know, but she was curious.

She decided to check out the truck for herself. But, as soon as she stepped onto the side of the road, Scoops barked in her arms. The next instant, he scrambled to the ground.

Alarm raced through her. "Scoops!"

The road beside them was busy, and her dog didn't need to be running around in this area. He could be hit by a car.

Thankfully, he ran into the woods rather than the road.

"Scoops!" Serena chased after him.

The last thing Serena wanted was to traipse around the wilderness getting ticks and poison ivy.

But for her dog, she'd take the risk.

As she followed Scoops, Elsa suddenly began playing another song: "Oh, Where Has My Little Dog Gone?"

Very funny, Serena mentally muttered. Glad to see that part of her truck had started working again.

She followed the dog between the short, stubby trees of the forest. These trees weren't meant to be walked through. They were thick barriers, protecting the island during storms. The underbrush and branches scratched her arms and ankles.

She didn't care.

"Scoops!" she called again, exasperation in her voice.

Her little dog kept running. These trees didn't bother that little guy one bit.

Serena, on the other hand, had at least a hundred twenty pounds on the dog. It wasn't nearly as easy for her to maneuver between the foliage.

As Serena hurried behind Scoops, something darted into her path.

She screamed, expecting the worst.

A rabid raccoon. A hungry fox. A coiled cottonmouth.

Then she realized it was just a wild turkey.

The bird gobbled away, unaffected by Serena.

Serena's hand remained over her heart as she willed her pulse to slow down.

Stupid wild turkey.

She'd heard the birds lived in these woods.

She'd just never run into one before. In the spring, people came to hunt them, just like they hunted the ducks of the waters of the Pamlico Sound.

After giving herself a moment to catch her breath, Serena continued through the woods.

Finally, she saw her dog stop at a spot just ahead.

"Scoops . . ." Serena shook her head, almost too out of breath to scold the dog.

Almost being the key word.

But the words she wanted to leave her mouth didn't.

Because Scoops was standing beside a body —a dead body with a gaping wound in his chest.

"WE'VE GOT to stop running into each other like this." Cassidy cast Serena a glance as they stood near the body in the woods.

Officers had strung crime-scene tape around the man. The medical examiner—Doc Clemson, who was also the island's doctor—stood over the victim, doing the initial examination. Cassidy had stepped back to give him space.

At one point in her life, Serena's curiosity and nosiness would have risen to the surface in this situation. But now she'd had enough. How many more dead bodies could she encounter this summer?

Cassidy swatted at a fly as they stood there. Tons of the insects swarmed around them—no doubt because of the corpse in the distance.

Serena felt nauseous thinking about it.

Thankfully, Webster had caught up with them and had taken Scoops back to the ice cream truck. It was one less thing Serena had to worry about.

"Have you ever seen this man before?" Cassidy asked.

"I didn't get a good look at him, but I'd definitely say no."

"How exactly did you find him again?"

"You wouldn't believe me if I told you," Serena said.

"Try me."

Serena ground her teeth together before explaining what had happened with Elsa and Scoops earlier.

Cassidy narrowed her eyes. "Very interesting."

Serena knew enough to know it wasn't a good sign when Cassidy said that. And, from the outside looking in, Serena had to agree. The way in which she'd found this body was highly suspicious.

Even more bothersome was the fact that her entire posse seemed to be working against her. First Elsa. Then Scoops.

At least Webster hadn't turned on her . . . yet.

"So you think this man was injured near my place and then somehow ended up in the woods on the other side of the campground?" Serena tried to picture it in her mind.

"I'd say it's a good possibility. When I looked at your place earlier, I didn't see any drag marks or signs of a scuffle. But somehow Elsa has blood on her."

"Maybe it wasn't this man's."

Cassidy raised her eyebrows. "You think two people were injured within the vicinity of your camper?"

That didn't sound any better, did it?

Serena shrugged. "I just don't want you to jump to any conclusions."

"Don't worry. I won't."

Serena swallowed hard, realizing her problems wouldn't be going away any time soon. "Do you need me to stay around any longer?"

"You're free to go. I know where to find you."

Serena started to step away but paused. "I'm telling you, Cassidy. I don't know anything about this. No matter how it might look."

Cassidy nodded before turning back to the crime scene.

A few moments later, Serena tromped back toward Elsa. She couldn't help but scowl at the vehicle as she passed in front of it. "Are you trying to get me in trouble?"

Elsa, of course, was quiet. But Serena couldn't help but think that her vehicle was betraying her somehow.

"I thought you were my friend," she muttered.

Maybe her truck was two-faced. Friendly and warm and inviting one minute and evil and malicious as soon as Serena turned her back.

That's right. Maybe her truck had a split personality.

Except vehicles didn't generally have personalities.

"Serena?"

She snapped out of her stupor and glanced

up at Webster. He must have seen her and climbed out from the front seat, Scoops in his arms.

She tried to compose herself. "Yes?"

"Are you okay? You're talking to your truck."

How much had she actually said out loud? Serena wasn't sure.

She laughed a little too self-consciously as she tried to brush it off. "Was I? Hmm . . . Anyway . . . I'm free to go, so I guess I'll head home. Did you call a tow truck?"

"I was in the process of doing so when Scoops ran away. I forgot about it until just now. Want me to try again?"

"Let me give the girl another chance," Serena said. "But if you'd wait for me, that would be great."

Elsa seemed to have a mind of her own. Most people might suspect cut brake lines, but not Serena. She had a feeling her truck had stopped here on purpose.

Not that that was possible.

But things like this always seemed to happen with Elsa.

Serena climbed into the driver's seat and cranked the engine.

To her surprise, Elsa purred to life, almost like nothing had happened.

"That's good news," Webster said as he stood beside her open door. "Is she safe to drive?"

"I'm not sure. But I'm willing to try." Truthfully, Serena didn't want to pay for a tow truck. And, in her gut, she had a feeling everything was going to be okay, that Elsa would cooperate.

"If you insist." Webster handed her Scoops and took a step back. "I'll follow you, just to make sure you get home safely."

Serena didn't argue. She welcomed Webster's company.

Because at the rate things were going today, who knew what might happen next?

Serena didn't even want to know.

CHAPTER FIVE

SERENA MENTALLY FUMED on the short drive back to her place.

Even though the thought was ridiculous, she still couldn't help but feel betrayed by her ice cream truck. Plus, she was on edge as she wondered if the brakes might go out again or if something else random might happen.

Thankfully, there were no other incidents for the rest of the drive.

She pulled up to her house, put Elsa in Park, and climbed out. She couldn't wait for some time by herself to think everything through and unwind.

Webster, to her surprise, met her near the

front door to her camper. "I should check things out before you go inside."

Serena realized he was just trying to be chivalrous. Even though Serena thought it was unnecessary, she nodded. Really, the notion was sweet.

"That would be great." She handed him her key.

She waited with Scoops as Webster disappeared inside her camper. There were very few places for anybody to hide in the compact space, so it was no surprise when he appeared back outside a few minutes later.

"It's all clear," Webster announced.

"That's good to know at least. Thank you."

Webster stood in front of her for another moment and opened his mouth like he wanted to say something.

There was something different in his gaze, she realized. What was it?

Serena wasn't sure. But she couldn't ignore the realization either.

Or maybe she could.

Her life was already complicated enough right now without trying to figure out what Webster was thinking.

"Listen, how about if I help you clean Elsa?" Webster finally said. "I assume you're going to want to get that blood off."

"Yes, I do need to do that, don't I?" Serena had already forgotten. "I'd love some help."

For the next hour, they washed her truck. Even Scoops joined them, playing in the spray from the hose. Serena turned on some music, and the lazy sounds of Jimmy Buffet stretched through the speakers.

When they finished, both Webster and Serena were wet. But the physical exertion had been therapeutic. If only it was as easy to wash the worry from her thoughts as it was to clean the stains from her truck.

After Serena put the hose away, she turned to Webster to say thank you. "You've been a huge help. I don't know how I can ever repay you."

"No repayment needed." Webster shrugged, as if it wasn't a big deal. "We still on for breakfast tomorrow morning at The Crazy Chefette?"

"I wouldn't miss it for the world."

A smile flashed across his face. "Great. I'll see you then."

With any luck, tomorrow things would start to feel normal again. Cassidy would realize that

Serena had nothing to do with this man's death. The real culprit would be apprehended. And Serena could continue to sell ice cream just like she always did.

Because some people said that love made the world go around.

But Serena was pretty sure it was actually ice cream.

———————

SERENA WOKE up at her normal time the next morning. As per her routine, she got dressed in her costume of the day.

Today, she'd decided to put on the persona of Alice from *Alice in Wonderland* so she could blend in with people at the children's festival. Even if she wouldn't be working at the event—not until Cassidy cleared her—it would be nice to feel a part of it.

Serena documented the process of transforming herself into the character, and then she posted it on all her social media accounts, where she had become something of an overnight sensation. Her subscriber count kept rising, much more rapidly than she'd ever dreamed.

She was getting more and more paid sponsorships from various makeup companies. But keeping up with all the comments and messages that people sent her was beginning to feel like a full-time job.

Could this ever become a full-time job for her? Would she want it to be?

Serena wasn't sure. She did love being an online influencer. And she was sure if she had more content to put out that her reach would grow even more.

But doing so would require cutting back on her ice cream and newspaper work. She also loved those things. She loved being out in public and interacting with people. She loved feeling like she was somehow making a difference, whether that was through brightening someone's day with a frozen treat or by bringing attention to an important issue through an article.

Decisions, decisions . . .

After she finished her post, she put Scoops on a leash, grabbed a poop bag, and shoved her phone in her pocket.

She headed to the beach for her morning walk, just as she did every day. It was good exercise and helped clear her head before the workday started.

The rest of the night had been uneventful. Serena had halfway expected Cassidy to show up again with some type of update or accusation. But that hadn't happened.

Just as the sun began to rise, Serena reached the location she'd been looking for.

She stopped in front of the seashell art that someone left on the beach each night. Serena still hadn't figured out who the artist was behind the wonderful designs. But whoever it was, he or she created masterful images that captured the imagination.

Today, the artist had crafted a beautiful mandala with perfectly symmetrical sides. The piece really was breathtaking.

Serena took several pictures to include with her article. BuzzFeed had recently picked up one of the pieces on the beach art, and it had gone viral. According to several people Serena had talked to, these creations had even begun bringing in new tourists who came just to see them.

Serena was glad she could do her part in helping to spread the news about what a great place Lantern Beach was. The island had experienced its fair share of troubles over the past couple of years, and she knew that many locals, including herself, depended on the revenue from tourist season to help pay their bills.

After she took her pictures, she and Scoops continued down the beach until they finally cut across the boardwalk, walked down the street, and into The Crazy Chefette.

The Crazy Chefette was Serena's favorite restaurant here on the island. Her friend Lisa Dillinger was the chef. The woman was a former chemist turned food inventor, as she called herself. She liked to experiment with unlikely taste combinations, which always made things interesting.

But lately, Lisa looked like she was ready to burst. Only one more month, and Lisa and her husband, Braden, would welcome their first baby.

As soon as Serena walked inside, the scent of bacon, fresh herbs, and coffee greeted her. She spotted Webster sitting at their usual booth. They got here early enough to miss most of the tourist crowd. That was good because it meant the two of them could sit in the same place each time.

Since Serena had brought Scoops when dogs weren't expressly allowed, she kept the dog near her feet and out of sight. She'd been doing it for the past month or so, and no one had said anything.

Serena smiled as she sat across from Webster, noting that he looked good today.

His skin was finally starting to get some sun. Some natural highlights had begun to appear in his dark hair. He'd even begun to loosen up on the way he dressed. No longer did he always wear his shirt tucked in or his pants perfectly ironed.

The urban outsider was finally adjusting to island life.

They ordered their normal breakfasts, and then Webster turned toward her. "Anything new?"

"No. I keep expecting to hear an update on yesterday's . . . situation, but I haven't heard a thing. You?"

"Unfortunately, no. I called Cassidy this morning to see if she could give me an update for an article, but she was tightlipped, as usual."

"The good news is I haven't been arrested yet." Serena shrugged, trying to look on the bright side.

"That *is* always good news."

Before they could talk any more, a shadow fell over the table. And the person that Serena saw standing there made her skin crawl.

CHAPTER SIX

SERENA STARED at the unruly little boy who'd discovered that blood on her truck as he stood beside her table. *Skippy*.

He stared at her now, his eyes narrowed suspiciously. "What are you doing here?"

"I always eat here," Serena told him. "You?"

"My mom made me come. I wanted to sleep in. I stayed up late last night playing video games, and I don't really care about breakfast. As far as I'm concerned, breakfast is for losers."

He really was a little ray of sunshine, wasn't he?

As Serena tried to unclench her jaw, she scanned the restaurant, searching for the boy's mom. She didn't see the weary woman anywhere.

"What are you doing today, bud?" Webster's voice sounded warm—and clueless. Did he not realize what a total brat this boy was? Or was he simply being a peacemaker right now?

"My mom's making me go back to that stupid children's festival. I really want to finish my Fortnite tournament. My squad is on fire right now."

"Aren't you too young to play that game?" Webster tilted his head.

"Aren't you too much of an inside boy to be living on the beach, you pale-faced namby-pamby?"

Serena's bottom lip nearly hit the floor. "Excuse me, but that was uncalled for. Don't you have a breakfast that you need to eat?"

Just as she said the words, the boy's mom appeared from around the corner. Her gaze darted around the restaurant before finally stopping on her son. She rushed toward him.

"Skippy! I'm gone to the bathroom for one minute, and you manage to sneak away again." She let out a fragile laugh, one also lined with exhaustion.

"Oh, Eloise. You're back. I was just talking to

the ice cream lady." Skippy turned back to Serena. "Have any more strawberry sauce?"

His words were not only pointed, but the boy sounded a little too satisfied as he said them.

Serena narrowed her gaze, a terse reply on the tip of her tongue. Before she could say anything she might regret, Skippy's mom put her hands on the boy's shoulders and turned him away.

"I told you—don't call me Eloise. It's disrespectful."

"It has a better ring to it than Mom."

"We'll talk more later." Eloise turned back to Serena. "Please don't mind him. He's been a little on edge lately. His dad is out to sea, and he acts up every time his father leaves."

As much as Serena wanted to be angry with the boy, her heart softened. Usually, beneath negative emotions and behaviors, there were deeper issues. She knew that. She'd experienced it in her own life.

But it was easy to forget sometimes when it came to working with difficult people.

As soon as Skippy walked away, Serena's phone buzzed. She glanced at the screen and saw she'd gotten some more comments and tags on social media.

Quickly, she clicked on them to check for anything timely she needed to respond to. One of the companies considering sponsoring her was supposed to be finalizing the deal today.

But when she clicked on one of her feeds, her eyes widened.

She saw a picture of a man. Wearing a red baseball cap. Standing in front of Elsa.

Serena sucked in a breath.

It was the dead man Serena had found yesterday.

What exactly was going on here?

"I THOUGHT I might find you here."

Serena knew exactly who'd spoken without looking up at the newest person who'd appeared beside her booth.

Cassidy Chambers.

Serena put her phone down so quickly that she nearly dropped it. She feared the police chief might see the photo and think Serena had something to do with that man's death.

Serena had nothing to do with it, though. For some reason, his image had shown up in her feed. She'd have to dig deeper into that fact in a moment—when Cassidy wasn't close enough to see over her shoulder.

"You were looking for me?" Serena's voice sounded thinner than she would've liked. She cleared her throat, vowing to do better, to sound less guilty.

Without invitation, Cassidy slid into the booth beside her. "You mind?"

"Of course not." Just as Serena said the words, her food was delivered—avocado toast for her and a yogurt parfait for Webster.

But Serena's appetite had disappeared faster than popsicles at a children's birthday party. She tried to take a sip of her coffee, but even that tasted acidic.

"Are you sure you don't know our dead man?" Cassidy studied Serena's face.

Serena felt the muscles in her throat tighten until she could hardly breathe. Licking her lips, she chose her words carefully. "I'm sure I've never met that man before. Why?"

Cassidy pulled out her phone. "Because we found the man's cell in the woods. It must have fallen out when his body was relocated. His wallet is missing, however. Anyway, we were able to break into the device, and we found some interesting pictures there."

"Is that right?" Serena felt the first wave of nausea hit her. This wasn't looking good, was it? How had she managed to find herself in the middle of another murder investigation? This time it was through absolutely no effort of her own.

Cassidy showed Serena a picture on her phone. "Recognize him?"

It was the same man with the red hat. The same photo Serena had seen online just moments earlier.

Her skin burned. "I don't."

"So why would he take a picture in front of your ice cream truck?" Cassidy continued.

"The man took a picture of your ice cream truck?" Webster frowned, pausing a spoonful of yogurt midair.

"I . . . don't know." Serena shrugged, knowing her jumpiness made her look guilty. "I really don't."

Cassidy and Webster both studied her face, not bothering to hide their scrutiny.

"Why do I feel like there's something that you're not telling me?" Cassidy shifted, resting her arm on the table as she turned toward Serena.

How much should she say? Serena cringed as she considered her next move. If she handled this wrong . . . her life could take a dramatically different turn.

In a split second, it felt like her future hinged on whatever she said next.

"Serena . . ." Warning laced Cassidy's voice as she waited.

"Okay, I'm kind of a social media sensation," Serena blurted. "I have accounts on all the major platforms, and I have thousands of followers. I've recently been highlighting Elsa in some of my photos, and she's also become somewhat of an overnight sensation. My only guess is that maybe this man tracked me down here so he could take a picture with Elsa. That's all I know. I promise."

The words came out so fast that even Serena hardly knew what she'd said.

Cassidy and Webster both stared at her, almost as if neither knew where to start. Or maybe their brains were still trying to catch up from what Serena called "Spiel in Double Time."

That had a nice ring to it, didn't it?

She set the thought aside.

"You're a social media sensation?" Cassidy finally said.

"I have almost a hundred thousand subscribers right now," Serena said. "I do little tutorials with my outfits and makeup. Just a few weeks ago, I started to include Elsa, and all of my fans *loved* it. My only guess is that this man may have been one of my fans."

Cassidy continued to stare.

"And I just so happened, right before you sat down, to check my social media updates. When I did, I saw that someone had tagged me in this random photo." She hit her screen and showed them the image she'd discovered. "This guy was in it."

"His photo?" Webster said.

Serena looked at the picture again. "It looks like his name is Jeremy Riser. He posted that picture yesterday, but one of his friends came back and tagged me in the post. That's why it just now showed up on my feed."

"What's the caption say?" Webster asked. "Anything?"

Serena read the words there. "He said: You'll

BANANA SPLIT PERSONALITIES   63

never believe who I just saw. If I'm lucky, maybe I'll meet I Am Quick Change too."

"I Am Quick Change?" Cassidy asked, her eyes narrowing with confusion.

"That's what I go by online. I didn't want to use my real name, and since I change my look daily, I thought it was appropriate."

"Interesting," Cassidy muttered.

"I may have mentioned Lantern Beach in one of my posts before, so it is viable that someone could've found me here," Serena continued.

"Has anything like this ever happened before?" Cassidy asked.

"No, I've gotten lots of strange messages. I've had some weird fans. But no one's ever actually tried to find me in real life."

"Is there anything else that you're not telling me?" Cassidy locked her gaze with Serena's.

"No, there's not. I promise. I literally just saw the photo seconds before you came and sat beside me."

"If you hear anything else, you will let me know."

Serena nodded. "I will. I promise."

But Serena didn't like the direction this was going.

CHAPTER SEVEN

"SO, YOU'RE AN INTERNET SENSATION, HUH?" Webster stared at Serena from across the table.

She almost didn't hear him. She was distracted by Lisa Dillinger—the owner of The Crazy Chefette. The woman stood behind the counter, muttering something about some missing cranberry and jalapeno muffins.

It seemed like sweet treats were disappearing from around town. First, Serena's ice cream sandwiches. Now Lisa's muffins.

Strange.

Serena remembered Webster's question and drifted back to the present. "Sorry. Internet sensation is probably an exaggeration."

"I think that's great. I'm surprised you haven't mentioned it before."

She shrugged again. "Sometimes it's nice to keep your private life private, you know? Things are simpler that way."

Maybe in some ways, Serena herself had a split personality. Her online persona versus her real-life persona. Her ice cream truck persona versus her journalist persona.

Everyone wore different hats in life, right? That didn't mean there was anything wrong with doing so. It just meant you were rising to the occasion.

That was Serena's opinion, at least, and she stood behind it.

"I can understand that," Webster said.

Before they could talk anymore, a new figure wandered to their table. Ethan Murphy, the coordinator of the children's festival. The man was in his mid-thirties, with light brown hair and a fit build. He seemed to be the epitome of brisk and professional—more New York elite than Lantern Beach homeboy.

Serena was pretty sure he worked out of Raleigh to schedule events like these.

He turned to Serena. "I was hoping I might run into you."

Serena pointed at herself. "Me?"

"Yes, you. Of course. Who else would I be talking about?" His words might have sounded sharp if he hadn't softened his voice.

"Why were you hoping to run into me?"

"I need you to come to the festival today and sell your banana splits."

"I'm not sure that's a good idea . . ." Serena didn't know how much the man knew about yesterday's events, nor did she want to fill him in on all the details while in public.

"I know about everything," he insisted, lowering his voice. "And I know you've been cleared. That's why I think it's a good idea to come back to the festival. What's the Beach, Books, and Banana Splits Children's Festival without banana splits?"

Serena rubbed the edge of her coffee mug as she contemplated his request. "I would need to check with the police chief before I promise anything."

"Do that and make sure she approves it. We need you there, ice cream lady."

"It's good to be needed, I suppose," Serena

said, still feeling hesitant. "But don't you think that people are going to be freaked out once they find out what happened?"

"Don't be silly. Tourists around here don't care about local news—only about their vacations. They'll never know."

"If you say so." But Serena wasn't so sure about that.

She had to admit that she could use the money from the festival—especially since all those bananas she'd purchased would go bad otherwise.

TWO HOURS LATER, Serena and Webster were back at the festival.

Cassidy had approved their participation and said she couldn't see any reason why they shouldn't be there.

Serena knew things wouldn't pick up until closer to lunchtime. Until then, she cleaned the inside of the ice cream truck and made sure that everything was in place for the big rush later. Her window was already open, and a pleasant breeze from the ocean floated inside.

As she looked outside, she saw the waves rolling in the distance. There was nothing like the sight of the ocean right outside the window. Something about it was soothing to the soul. Mix that with the happy songs playing in the distance, and this seemed like an idyllic moment.

As Serena stared out, a new voice floated inside.

She recognized it as the director's, Ethan Murphy.

He stood near the woman who played the ukulele. The two of them appeared to be arguing about something, and neither seemed to be backing down.

"What do you think is going on over there?" Webster stood beside Serena at the window, staring with interest at the argument.

"Who knows?" Serena shrugged. "I wonder if you have to be high-strung to organize something like this. Does it come with the territory?"

"I've seen plenty of people operate with grace under pressure," Webster said. "Maybe he's new at doing this or something. This is the first time you guys have had this event here, right?"

"That's right. My understanding is that Ethan

approached Lantern Beach about coming here. I can see why. This island has a great history full of pirates and treasure and shipwrecks. What's there not to love about coming to a place like this? Plus, I know the tourism board was all in favor."

"They always are."

As Ethan walked away, the ukulele player wandered to the ice cream truck. "I think I need an ice cream sundae."

"I can help you with that," Serena grabbed a bowl while Webster began to scoop some ice cream. "Everything okay over there?"

"Ethan's just being Ethan." The woman waved her hand in the air. "It's my fault, really. He caught me smoking behind one of the buildings. He said I wasn't setting a good example."

Serena couldn't argue that.

"He's all about image. Before he worked as an event planner, he was a publicist—the type who did damage control. If you were a CEO who got your company bad press? Ethan was your guy. He even worked with celebrities and professional ball players. What do you call people with that job? Fixers? That's what he was."

Serena stored that information away as she

handed the woman her ice cream. "Here you go. I hope your day gets better."

"Me too. I just need a nicotine patch."

As she left, somebody else walked up to the window.

"You want a banana split?" Serena started, snapping back into saleswoman mode. "They're really lit. We've got it all, from big or small. Chocolate or vanilla? Maybe you'd like it all together."

Serena had just come up with that rhyme, and it was one of her better ones, if she did say so herself.

"Are you I Am Quick Change?" The teen stared up at Serena with bright, curious eyes.

Serena's cheeks heated. She rubbed her neck as a sudden ache appeared. "Why would you ask that?"

"My friend and I follow you on Insta," the young woman rushed, calling one of her companions over. "We just love your stuff. We heard that you lived here, so we thought it would be fun to find you. Is it okay if we get our pictures with you and Elsa?"

Serena didn't know quite what to say. She'd spent months building up her online presence.

But in person fame? That seemed like a totally different story.

"Sure," she finally said, though somewhat reluctantly.

She leaned out the window and smiled as the two girls took a picture with her.

As they walked away, she heard them muttering, "Wait until we tell all our friends. They're not going to believe this."

Serena wasn't sure that was going to be a good thing . . . especially given what was going on here lately.

She just might need to hire Ethan to fix things for her also.

CHAPTER EIGHT

YESTERDAY'S CRIME hadn't slowed down business. The day so far had been hopping, and Serena was running out of bananas, believe it or not.

She knew one thing for sure. When this was over, she would be ready to get off her feet and rest for a bit.

Before she could do that, Cassidy appeared again.

Normally, Serena was happy to see the woman. But not today. And especially not when Serena saw the police chief's eyes.

Cassidy obviously had an update, and Serena wasn't sure she was prepared for it.

"I just thought you'd want to hear the latest."

Cassidy leaned into the window where Serena sold ice cream. "The particulates on Elsa's grill matched the blood type of the man we found in the woods."

Serena's throat tightened. "Did they?"

"There's one other thing I thought I would share with you." Cassidy looked around to make sure there were no listening ears. "It looks like the man was killed with a bow and arrow."

"What?" The word came out fast as surprise filled her.

Cassidy nodded. "It's true. That's why no one heard a gunshot. But the arrow went right through him, and we haven't been able to find it anywhere. That most likely means that the killer grabbed it."

Serena's hands went to her hips. "So, this man took a picture with Elsa. While he was still standing there, someone tracked him down, shot him with an arrow, and then dragged his body through the woods?"

"The arrow went right through his heart," Cassidy said. "He died instantaneously."

"That's still horrible."

"It is," Cassidy agreed.

Serena shifted her jaw with thought. "What kind of killer uses a bow and arrow?"

"You've got me. This is a first for me." Cassidy narrowed her gaze as she stared at Serena. "You don't own one, do you?"

"Of course not." Serena halfway felt insulted that Cassidy even had to ask.

"One more question. Tell me again where you were between seven and eight o'clock on the night of the murder?"

"She was with me." Webster appeared beside Serena. "Several people saw us walking on the beach together. The weather cooled down some, and it seemed like everyone in town went out to enjoy it."

Cassidy nodded. "I need to double-check with a couple of people, just to keep things on the up and up."

"Of course," Serena said. "I'm assuming that was Jeremy Riser's time of death?"

"It was. If you hear anything else, let me know." And with that, Cassidy walked away.

Serena glanced at Webster after she left. "Things just keep getting weirder and weirder."

"You can say that again," Webster muttered.

"I hadn't seen weird until I came to Lantern Beach."

AT FIVE O'CLOCK, Serena closed up shop. She still had other work she needed to get done, like for the newspaper. But what she really wanted was a long, hot bath.

Which she wouldn't get because she didn't have a bathtub in her camper.

She was going to have to settle for a long, hot shower instead.

But her feet felt surprisingly achy. She wasn't used to being on them all day, not like she had been the past two days.

Serena left her ice cream truck parked at the festival since there was one more day until it ended. Webster offered to give her and Scoops a ride home. As soon as she climbed into his air-conditioned vehicle, she felt herself relax.

Hopefully, Cassidy was tracking down some leads. For all she knew, the police chief could have this man's killer in custody.

And Serena's conscience would be clear

because she honestly had no idea who he was or why someone killed him.

Nor could Cassidy possibly think that she had anything to do with his death. She was accounted for during the time when he died.

"What a day, huh?" Webster said as he pulled to a stop in front of her camper.

"You can say that again," Serena told him. "Thanks for being there for me. I really appreciate it."

"Let me walk you up."

Before she could refuse, he'd taken off his seatbelt and hurried out the door.

Moments later, the two of them stood facing each other on her little porch. Scoops sat at their feet, almost as if anticipating whatever might happen next.

Just like last night, as Serena stared at Webster, she felt something changing inside her.

It made no sense. She couldn't possibly *like* Webster. He wasn't her type. And she wasn't even really looking for a relationship.

So why did she have the overwhelming urge to reach up and kiss him?

She flinched and put the idea out of her head.

But was Webster thinking the same thing?

Based on the look in his eyes . . . maybe.

And that was just weird. The two of them were simply friends.

She wasn't looking for romance—or to have her heart broken again when she made the wrong decision. She'd carefully built up the walls around herself to ensure that didn't happen.

She waited, sensing Webster was about to say something deep and meaningful. Instead, he said, "Serena . . ."

"Yes?"

"Your door is cracked open."

"My door is . . ." She looked over, and her eyes widened at the confirmation. "That's weird."

"Stay here while I check it out." Webster's voice left no room for argument.

The next instant, he disappeared inside.

She knew something was wrong when she heard him say, "What do you think you're doing in here?"

CHAPTER NINE

SERENA COULDN'T WAIT any longer. She pulled the door open and peered inside.

She sucked in a quick breath at what she saw there.

"Skippy?" The word sounded raw as it left her lips.

He sat on the couch inside Serena's camper, a bag of potato chips in his hand.

"What are you doing here?" Serena stepped into her space and stared at the intruder.

As she did, someone ran up behind her. "Is Skippy...?"

Serena turned to see Eloise standing there, clearly out of breath and worried.

Serena stepped back so the woman could see her son sitting on the couch.

"Oh, Skippy . . ." Eloise's shoulders hunched with unmistakable disappointment. "What are you thinking?"

Skippy shrugged as if he didn't have a care in the world and bite into another chip, leaving crumbs everywhere.

Serena remembered the dead man outside her camper and knew that she needed to proceed with caution. She probably should even call Cassidy.

But, despite how guilty Skippy looked, Serena really couldn't see the boy—or his mom—being a killer. Then again, maybe that fact would make them the best suspects yet.

"I'm not sure what got into Skippy." Eloise rubbed her hands on her shorts as if trying to ward away her nerves. "The two of us decided to go on a bike ride, and I could hardly keep up with Skippy. I saw him veering this direction, and then when I remembered he'd seen the ice cream truck last night . . . I put two and two together."

Serena's gaze went to Skippy. "How did you know where I lived?"

"You can see the ice cream truck from the road if you look really hard. Duh!" Skippy shrugged, not a hint of remorse in his eyes. "I saw it earlier, and I wanted to come to check your place out."

"And why would you do that?" This boy was making no sense.

"I thought you might have more ice cream here. Instead, I had to settle for potato chips."

"What?" Serena's voice rose an octave with surprise. "What would give you that idea?"

"You have to keep your extra inventory somewhere."

"So you broke into my camper?" Serena asked, trying to follow his line of thought.

"I learned how to pick locks online. Really isn't that hard." He looked satisfied as his lips tugged at the corners.

"Did you break into the truck yesterday? Some ice cream sandwiches are missing."

He just grinned.

He was a little thief, wasn't he? A robber and a thief.

For that matter, was he the one who took the muffins from The Crazy Chefette?

That was Serena's best guess.

Scoops barked at Skippy as if he didn't approve of the boy's actions either.

"I didn't see a bike outside," Webster said.

"I left it behind the camper," Skippy said. "Not on purpose. It was just the easiest way to get to the camper from the road."

Not comforting.

"So you got in here, discovered I had no ice cream stored in this small space, and then decided to make yourself comfortable?" Serena clarified.

Who did that?

"I'd just walked in when I got caught," Skippy said. "Thankfully you left these chips out, at least."

As Serena stood there, she tried to ascertain whether or not he was telling the truth. She saw nothing in the boy's body language to indicate he was lying. Skippy's mom looked truly remorseful, and Skippy was making no apologies for what he'd done.

"I won't press charges—this time." Serena latched her gaze onto Skippy's. "But I don't ever want to catch you breaking into my property again, understand?"

Skippy nodded. "Understood."

"ONE MORE WEIRD event to add to our day," Webster said after Skippy and his mom left.

"Did you believe them?" Serena sat on her hammock with Scoops, enjoying a balmy breeze, while Webster sat in a chair across from her.

"I did. But if there's anything I've learned about crime, it's that you should trust but verify."

"Agreed." Serena sighed and leaned back, staring at the sky as it began to turn a lovely shade of pinkish gray. "I'm not pressing charges, but I am going to call Cassidy and let her know what's going on—just in case."

"Probably a good idea." Webster shifted. "What are you thinking about now?"

"I'm just trying to picture it all playing out," Serena said. "I'm picturing this Jeremy Riser guy coming by my place and taking a photo with Elsa. I'm visualizing him being shot with a bow and arrow. I'm imagining his body being dragged through the woods to a different spot."

"And?"

"The drag marks were covered up, and no one saw anything. It's like the person who did this was a ghost, and it's just all unnerving.

Then finding Skippy in my camper just now . . ."

"That was unsettling." Webster shrugged. "I guess it's like my mom always used to say: be careful what you wish for."

Serena studied him, not completely sure what he meant. "What are you getting at?"

"I mean, I don't know if you've always wanted to be famous or not. But now that you've made a name for yourself, people are starting to seek you out. That can create a whole different level of upheaval in your life. If you like privacy, you can kiss it goodbye."

She stroked Scoops and frowned as she considered Webster's words. "What I really wanted was to show people how to put together makeup and costumes. When I started to get sponsorships, that was the icing on the cake."

Webster offered a compassionate smile. "I'm sure this will pass. Besides, Lantern Beach is so far away that it's not like people can just jump in their cars on the spur of the moment and come here."

Serena nodded. "You're right. They can't. They would need to plan. And, even if they did that, there would be no guarantees that they would find me here, right?"

Webster glanced at the spot where Elsa normally sat in front of her camper. "If a ten-year-old boy can spot Elsa from the road and realize where you live, I'm sure other people would be able to do that too."

Serena frowned. Maybe she needed to think of somewhere else to park Elsa. At least, for a while.

Just then, her phone buzzed. When she looked down, she saw that a potential social media sponsor had sent her a message. It was a reminder about the moral clause in the contract, and it ensured that Serena didn't do anything to bring bad publicity to their company.

Her eyes widened as she thought that through.

If Jeremy Riser's death was tied to Serena, could these companies drop her?

They couldn't do that, could they?

Serena knew the truth. They could do anything they wanted.

But Serena depended on every little bit of money she earned to help pay her bills. If she dropped even one of the balls she juggled, she'd be in a world of financial hurt.

Even more than before, Serena realized she had to help find this killer and turn this narrative around before even more lives were ruined.

CHAPTER TEN

THE NEXT MORNING, Serena stared at her phone, at the picture of Jeremy Riser as he stood in front of Elsa. Nausea squeezed her stomach.

The man looked so happy as he posed there in his bathing suit, T-shirt, and red baseball cap. His grin was wide. His hand was posed in a "hang loose" sign.

How had the moment turned so violent?

Serena had spent most of the night doing research on the man. She'd hoped to discover an interesting clue about him that would show her why he was killed.

But she didn't. There were no nasty notes posted on his social media. No snide comments. No malicious exes.

The man seemed normal.

He was twenty-six. A web designer. From Cincinnati, Ohio.

Based on Jeremy's social media posts, he'd come to Lantern Beach with his girlfriend. They'd been looking forward to their first vacation together. The pictures of the two of them together made them seem happy. He'd simply called her Khya, but he hadn't linked to her profile.

Though mostly women followed Serena, she did have a few males who actively engaged with her on social media. Strangely enough, as she'd looked back through all her old posts, Jeremy's name hadn't popped up.

In some ways, that proved to Serena that he hadn't been a superfan.

Had he come here knowing Serena lived on the island?

No doubt, Cassidy was looking into those details. Maybe the police chief would share some of that information with Serena. It was doubtful, but a girl could hope.

In between doing this research, Serena had finalized her article on the beach art. She'd also planned out her outfits for the upcoming week and had played with some new slogans she'd use while selling ice cream.

Finally, sometime in the middle of the night, she'd drifted to sleep on her couch, hugging the notebook where she'd jotted her ideas.

When she woke up, she realized she'd overslept. Serena was going to have to skip her walk this morning if she wanted to do her social media posts. It was either one or the other.

She glanced at her watch. Thankfully, she and Webster weren't meeting for breakfast this morning. They'd agreed they couldn't afford to do so every morning—because of their wallets and their waists.

Working quickly, she began to get ready for her day.

Today's persona: Pippi Longstocking.

Serena had found the perfect outfit at a thrift store. She'd only had to make a few changes to the sack-like dress to transform it. She also figured out a way to maneuver some wire into her braids. The strands now stood out from either side of her head.

She glanced in the mirror and smiled. She'd achieved the look she'd been going for.

A few minutes later, she had everything

posted online. But, before leaving her camper, she took a moment to check her messages.

Dread pooled in her stomach as she waited. She feared she might see something else that would implicate her in a murder.

To her relief, there was nothing out of the ordinary. No sponsors had dropped her either.

She counted her blessings for that, yet she knew it wasn't too late for things to go south. Things could turn around, and they could turn around quickly.

That seemed to be her life story.

Serena glanced at the time once more.

She had to get to the children's festival. Today was the last day, and she needed to double-check all her supplies to make sure she was well stocked before it started. A new order of bananas was supposed to be waiting for her at the grocery store.

Now, Serena just prayed for no more unexpected surprises.

A COUPLE OF HOURS LATER, Serena was successfully selling banana splits at the children's festival, again with Webster by her side.

The crowds didn't seem to be tired yet from all the activities. Today, the town librarian read some of her favorite books on a nearby swing while children sat around her. Several authors had also come in to do readings. Serena's favorite was the woman who had written *Lickity Split, Who Said Bananas Spit?* By the time the woman finished her reading, Serena had worked for several hours nonstop serving up her frozen treats.

In fact, her arm was beginning to ache from scooping ice cream, and she had only enough bananas left to maybe serve thirty more people.

Despite everything that happened, Serena would deem this event to be an overall success.

Maybe a person with Ethan's high-strung personality was just the type of guy you needed to organize an event like this. It had gone off without a hitch . . . mostly.

Serena rubbed her aching hands, grateful for a brief break between customers. But just as she did that, a woman around Serena's age appeared at her window. Based on her narrowed eyes, she wasn't very happy.

"Can I help you?" Serena started.

"*You're* I Am Quick Change?" the woman gaped as she stared at Serena.

"I am."

"You're so not that impressive in person."

Serena shrugged, feeling like a nasty online troll had materialized in real life.

She raised her chin, not giving this woman the satisfaction of a face-to-face thumbs down. "I resemble that remark. Who are you?"

The woman's eyes narrowed even more. "I'm Jeremy Riser's girlfriend, and I'm here to find out if you killed him."

CHAPTER ELEVEN

"YOU'RE WHO?" Serena stared at the woman, certain that she hadn't heard correctly.

"My name is Khya. Khya Smith. I came here on vacation with Jeremy Riser."

Realization swept through Serena. She'd seen her picture on Jeremy's social media, only this woman had a different haircut now. "I'm so sorry for your loss."

A moment of grief flooded in Khya's gaze, followed by a flash of anger. "He came here because he was obsessed with you, you know?"

Heat rose on Serena's cheeks. "I never met him."

Khya didn't seem to hear Serena. "He didn't

tell me this was why he picked Lantern Beach, but now everything makes sense."

"Like I said, I never met him," Serena continued. "I'm really sorry about what happened to him. It was tragic."

Khya's eyes narrowed even more, her anger continuing to grow. "If he hadn't started following you online, he'd still be alive right now."

"I . . . don't know what to say." For once in her life, Serena was at a loss for words. Khya's statement felt like a slap in the face—an undeserved slap.

Khya stepped closer and narrowed her eyes until she looked almost snakelike—which could be precisely the effect she was going for. "You should know I've already started a smear campaign against you. Everyone is going to know what you did."

"But I didn't do anything!" Serena's voice rose. This woman couldn't be serious, could she?

"It doesn't matter what you did or didn't do. What matters is what people *think* that you did." Khya's voice rose with excitement—and vengeance.

"Why would you want to ruin me?" This still wasn't making any sense.

"Because from the moment Jeremy watched your very first video, you ruined my life. I know he had a crush on you. I just know it."

"Maybe he just wanted to design my website or something . . ." Serena suggested.

"That's ludicrous." Khya shook her head. "My video channel isn't as popular as yours—I only have thirty thousand followers. But they're very loyal."

"You have a vlog? You don't even have a social media account."

Her eyes narrowed. "So you do know who I am . . ."

"Only because I researched Jeremy this morning, and I saw you in some of his photos."

"I don't use my real name. I like to keep things separate. My public name is Kindred."

"Kindred?" Serena repeated.

"It's a one-word name—like Madonna. People are going to remember it one day. I don't do makeup or costumes like you do, but my fans watch me open boxes all day."

"What in the world are you talking about?"

"I order gadgets, open them, and then show my

viewers what they look like. I give them my reaction, and they tell me whether we're kindred spirits or not—hence the name. And we're almost always kindred spirits, which is why they're so loyal to me."

"Interesting."

"All I've got to say is watch out because I'm going to be unboxing you next."

With that statement, Khya turned on her heel and hobbled away.

Serena felt stunned as she stood there, trying to process exactly what had just happened.

It looked like she really might need to hire Ethan Murphy to clean up lies about her.

As if she could afford that . . .

―――――――――

"ARE YOU OKAY?" Webster asked.

Serena had forgotten that he was in the truck with her. Everything else had faded except for Khya's words.

"I don't know," Serena admitted, leaning against the counter where she served ice cream. "It sounds like that woman has started a campaign to try to cancel me for something I didn't do—and for something I had no control over."

Webster's hand went to Serena's shoulder, and he gave it a comforting squeeze. "It's not right when people do something like that. I'm so sorry."

Serena shook her head, still in shock over the conversation. "Me too. I just . . . I can't believe this."

"You know what I think?" Webster said.

Serena looked up, curious about the hope in his voice. "What's that?"

"Who's the first person the police always look at in these circumstances?"

Realization washed through her. "The spouse or the boyfriend/girlfriend."

Webster pointed at Serena. "Exactly. If this Khya woman was in town when Jeremy was killed . . . I think she should be the first suspect. Maybe she's trying to deflect any potential attention off herself."

"You know what? You're right." His words made a lot of sense.

"Of course I'm right," Webster said. "I didn't graduate at the top of my class for nothing."

Despite herself, Serena smiled. "I'm glad I met you, Webster Newsome."

"Same here, Serena Lavinia. Now it looks like you need to get busy if we want to learn more about Khya Smith."

CHAPTER TWELVE

"KHYA SMITH WAS at Lantern Beach Medical Clinic most of the evening during the time when Jeremy died." Serena frowned and shook her head as she lowered her phone. "I talked to the nurse who works at the reception desk and promised her free ice cream. She said the woman went for a walk alone on the beach and cut her foot on a broken bottle."

"She told you that? Sharing that kind of information isn't legal, is it?"

"Probably not. The nurse actually didn't give any names. But it was Khya. She didn't kill Jeremy."

"So we're back at square one?"

Serena frowned and nodded. "That's how it looks."

The two of them sat in Elsa with the AC blaring. They'd officially closed up shop. But, instead of leaving this area to do their investigating, both she and Webster had pulled out their phones and got right to work.

That work consisted of internet searches and phone calls.

"I think we should think this through some more," Webster continued. "Jeremy and his girlfriend came here alone. They didn't know anyone else. They'd just arrived the morning of the day Jeremy died."

"Okay . . ." Serena waited for him to get to his point.

"It seems unlikely that someone followed him here and killed him," Jeremy continued. "But there is a possibility that he wandered into something that he shouldn't have."

"Like a drug deal maybe?"

Webster nodded. "Exactly. Or a theft. The crime could have been random—it may have been a matter of him being in the wrong place at the wrong time."

She thought back to her neighbors. Could one of them have been up to no good?

Or what about Skippy? She didn't see the ten-year-old as a killer. But what if his sticky fingers had been at work near the trailer?

Serena shook her head. Even if that had happened, there was no way Skippy could have dragged the man through the woods.

"Don't give up hope, Serena." Webster turned toward her, his voice filled with concern and encouragement. "You'll find answers. You always do."

Her heart lifted at his kind words. "Thanks for believing in me, Webster. I appreciate it."

Their gazes locked, and that strange emotion passed between them again. What was going on? Why did that keep happening? It made no sense.

"What now?" Webster asked.

"That's a good question. So far, my two main suspects are a little ten-year-old boy and his mom —and I really don't think they did it—or a girl-friend with an alibi. Neither look very promising."

Webster leaned back in his seat, almost as if a thought had settled on him. "You know what I'm curious about? The bow and arrow. It's not something that most people just happen to have on them."

"But there *are* enthusiasts who like to play around with them."

"This would have to be a pretty high-powered bow to send an arrow straight through Jeremy's heart and kill him. I don't know a ton about bows, but I know enough."

His words made sense. But Serena wasn't sure how that helped their case right now. "There's really no way to find out who in this area might have a bow like that. I'm not sure how much Cassidy has discovered, but I just don't even know how to figure out who might be behind this."

Webster squeezed her arm, as if sensing her discouragement. "You really think you're going to lose that many followers over this?"

"Have you seen some of those smear campaigns that have gone viral? Other bloggers and vloggers can be vicious. If they have a chance to tear me down because they think they might get a few more followers for themselves? They'll do it. They won't even think twice."

"And here I thought that journalism was a dog-eat-dog world."

"It seems like the whole world has gone crazy sometimes, doesn't it?"

"Yes, sometimes it does. Listen, since we're finished here, why don't we go hang out at your place?"

"Don't you have an article to work on?" Serena asked, surprised that the workaholic didn't want to get back to his office.

"There's nothing that can't wait until either later tonight or tomorrow. I say we have a little bonfire and try to take it easy. You've been working hard. You deserve it."

"Then why not?"

───────────

SERENA STARED at the tongues of fire as they reached toward the sky. Something about watching the flames flickering inside the brick firepit mesmerized her and temporarily swept her away from all her problems.

And that was a big task within itself.

She and Webster sat beside each other on little camping chairs Serena had pulled from a shed behind her place. A smoky scent surrounded them, and the sound of crickets in the nearby woods added pleasant sensory elements to the peaceful moment.

Serena glanced at Webster as he poked the fire with a stick he'd found in the woods. He seemed just as mesmerized by the flames as she did.

"Have you ever dated anyone seriously?" Serena didn't know where the question had come from, but she wanted to know. Webster never talked about that part of his life.

"There was one girl I got pretty serious with back in Richmond. But when everything went down there after that exposé I wrote, she dropped me like a sack of hot potatoes."

Webster had written an article exposing poor working conditions at a nearby factory. Instead of helping the cause, several people—innocent people—had been fired. He'd tried to do the right thing, but he'd gotten the wrong results.

Serena frowned. "I'm sorry. That couldn't have been easy."

"It wasn't. But at least I saw her true colors when I did."

"That's one way to look on the bright side."

Webster stole a glance at Serena. "How about you?"

She drew in a long breath as she quickly reflected on her dating life. "Nothing too serious. Well, I suppose that's not true. I dated the same guy for about two years back in Michigan."

"I'd say that was serious."

"It might sound that way, but it wasn't. The two of us were friends, and we thought it made sense to date. But even when we were dating, we really felt more like friends."

Webster leaned forward, the campfire warming his features. "So why'd you break up?"

"I decided to move to Lantern Beach. When I decided to leave, we both knew that things were over. There were no hard feelings, and we're still friends." As she said the words, her throat tightened. That wasn't the complete truth. But . . . Serena just couldn't bring herself to share all of those details.

"I think it says a lot about a person when you can still be friends with your ex even after you've broken up."

"Aunt Skye always tells me that the best relationships start out as friendships." Serena clamped her mouth shut. She hadn't been trying to imply anything about her and Webster when she said that. She hoped Webster didn't jump to that conclusion.

"I'm inclined to agree." Webster nodded slowly. "Sometimes, I think I'm ready to settle down, even though some people might say I'm too young."

She stared at his profile a moment. "You're twenty-six, right?"

"I am. But a lot of people my age are waiting until they're closer to thirty to even think about marriage. But I don't see what's so great about being single, especially if you find someone that you want to spend the rest of your life with."

His words caused a warm, sweet feeling to spread through her chest. "I'm twenty-three. Sometimes I feel ancient, and other times I feel like I should still be in junior high. Several of my friends from high school are already married. A few of them already have kids even. That's a little hard for me to imagine. But they seem happy. Really happy."

"Life is what you make of it. You can be single and happy, and you can be married and happy. Each of those have their challenges and rewards."

She studied his face another moment—the

strong lines of his profile, the slight upheaval of his normally neat hair, the gentle muscles rippling beneath the sleeves of his T-shirt.

"Do you see yourself staying here in Lantern Beach for a while?" she asked.

He shrugged, still staring at the fire. "I like it here. It surprised even me. But this place has a lot of charm, and it's a great community. If the death rate could just go down a bit, that might be a little better."

"At least, we always have something to write about."

"I can't argue about that." He chuckled before glancing at Serena. "I have to admit that part of the reason it's been so nice to come here is because of you, Serena."

The warm and sweet feeling continued to grow in Serena's chest like a melted marsh-mallow waiting for some chocolate and graham crackers. "That's really nice of you, Webster."

"I mean it. You surprised me. In a good way."

As she studied him, she found herself smiling. "You surprised me too, Webster."

Their gazes latched for a moment.

Was it just Serena's imagination or were they leaning toward each other?

Based on the smoky look in Webster's eyes, he was thinking about kissing her.

And Serena was thinking about kissing him too.

But, before their lips connected, Scoops sprang from Serena's lap. He took off toward something in the distance, snapping them out of their moment.

Serena released her breath, breaking their magnetic-like locked gazes. Instead, her eyes trailed her little dog.

Where had Scoops gone now?

And could his timing be any worse?

CHAPTER THIRTEEN

"WHAT IS it with Scoops running away from you lately?" Webster asked as they chased the little furball behind several campers.

"Good question. He's usually content to stay right at my side."

Serena's heart still pounded in her chest. She'd been anticipating that kiss more than she realized. Truthfully, she was a little cranky it had been interrupted.

Still, she couldn't be mad at Scoops. The dog had saved her life on more than one occasion, so she'd let this little indiscretion pass just for that reason.

She pulled up the flashlight on her phone so she could see where she was going. It was dark outside now, and, though the area was generally safe, the occasional water moccasin did call this island home. A few rattlesnakes had even been spotted this year.

"Scoops!" Serena called.

The dog continued to bounce ahead, as if on a mission. What had he heard or seen?

As they reached a puddle of marshy water, Serena paused.

"Here, let me help you." Webster reached for her hand. As she slipped her fingers in between his, a bolt of electricity shot through her.

A bolt of electricity? It sounded so cliché. But that was the only way she could think to describe that feeling.

As she hopped over the puddle and onto the other side, Webster didn't let go of her hand.

And Serena didn't complain. She liked the feeling of her fingers between his. It made her feel stronger, she supposed.

"Scoops!" Webster called.

The dog still hurried away.

Serena just prayed that he didn't find another dead body. She wished she could say that was out of the realm of possibility. However, that wasn't her experience.

Finally, Scoops stopped behind a neighbor's camper. The canine sat at attention and waited for Serena and Webster to catch up.

Serena had a bad feeling about this.

As she reached the dog, she squatted to look at him eye to eye. "What were you thinking, boy?"

Scoops took a step back and barked at something behind the camper.

As he did, Serena glanced at a wheelbarrow situated there.

She shone her flashlight inside.

A baseball cap lay on the rusty metal bed.

A red one.

Just like the one Jeremy Riser had been wearing in that photo right before he died.

SERENA TRIED NOT to listen as Cassidy questioned thirtysomething Kevin Bardsley in front of his camper. But she and Webster stood on the edge of the man's property, just close enough to overhear their conversation.

And Serena wasn't complaining.

"Are you telling me you've never seen this

man?" Cassidy clarified, holding up her phone.

No doubt, there was a photo of Jeremy Riser there.

"That's right," Kevin said, each syllable sounding like a grunt. "I've never seen him."

"Then explain how his hat got into your wheelbarrow."

"I'm telling you. I have no idea how it got there. No idea." He sliced his hands through the air a little too adamantly.

Kevin was one of the locals that Webster had talked about earlier. The man was a surfer who had no qualms about living the stereotypical surfer's lifestyle. In fact, even right now as the man spoke with the police chief, he acted high. He smelled high. A haze came from his trailer.

None of those things screamed "upstanding citizen."

"I'm going to need to check out the inside of your trailer." Cassidy took a step toward the man's camper.

Kevin practically jumped in front of her. "You don't want to do that."

Cassidy's hands went to her hips as she looked up at him. "And why is that?"

"It's . . . I don't know, man. It's a . . . mess."

She tried to step past him. "I don't mind messes."

Again, Kevin blocked her. "No, really. It's *very* messy."

Cassidy paused and stared him down. "What are you hiding inside your house, Kevin? A bow and arrow?"

"A bow and arrow? Why would I have a bow and arrow?" His grunts turned into fast-paced, slurred words instead.

"For the same reason you have a dead man's hat in the wheelbarrow."

"I'm telling you, I didn't kill that man." He sliced his hands through the air again.

"But have you ever talked to him?"

"I did see him wandering around here a few nights ago. But that's it."

Cassidy raised her head, looking more irritated by the moment. "You're going to need to start talking."

"It's all kind of a blur."

I wonder why that is, Serena thought, adding a mental eye roll.

"We can do this the easy or the hard way," Cassidy continued.

Finally, Kevin stepped back and let out a

resigned sigh. Officer Leggott lingered near Cassidy's SUV, monitoring the situation while Cassidy stepped into Kevin's trailer.

Serena waited, wondering if the police chief would find anything. Wondering if this was all too easy.

But when Cassidy finally emerged twenty minutes later, Serena immediately saw the satisfied look on her face.

She found something. Serena was sure of it.

The question was, was it enough to pinpoint him as the killer?

CHAPTER FOURTEEN

"THIS IS JEREMY RISER'S WALLET." Cassidy held something up in an evidence bag. "Do you mind telling me where you got it?"

"I don't know what you're talking about." Kevin took a step back and shrugged, raising his hands in the air as if to drive home the point.

"I think you do." Cassidy eyed him. "You're going to have to come down to the station with me."

Kevin stared at her. The next instant, the man took off in a run.

He only made it three steps when Webster extended his leg and tripped him.

Kevin landed in the little puddle that Webster had helped Serena step over earlier.

Cassidy pulled the man to his feet and hand-cuffed him, before leading him to her SUV.

"Good work, guys," she called over her shoulder.

Once Kevin was snuggly situated in the back of her vehicle, Cassidy put her phone to her ear. Probably calling for backup, if Serena had to guess. The rest of this guy's house needed to be thoroughly searched.

But maybe there would finally be an end to all this madness.

A girl could hope, at least.

SERENA LOOKED up at Webster as they stood on her deck thirty minutes later. After all that had happened, the earlier moment between them had been broken.

Was there a way to pick up where they'd left off? And was that really what Serena wanted?

She licked her lips as she looked up at Webster. "Smooth move back there, tripping Kevin like you did. Good job."

"Maybe we should be telling Scoops good job." Webster leaned down and gave the dog, who sat at Serena's feet, a hearty pat on the head.

She smiled. "Maybe we should."

He straightened, and his eyes met hers. His whole demeanor changed from Sweet Dog Whisperer to Possible Prince Charming. "Listen, Serena—"

Before Webster could finish that thought, his phone rang. He glanced at the screen and frowned. "It's my aunt. She needs me to pick up her allergy medicine on the way home. Apparently, she can't stop sneezing today."

Serena's heart sank with disappointment. What was he about to say?

"I understand," she finally said.

Webster seemed to reluctantly take a step back. "Tomorrow?"

"I'll see you then."

"And Serena." Webster paused and looked back at her. "Everything's going to be okay. I wouldn't worry about that Khya woman. Your true fans are going to see right through her."

Serena's spirits lifted at his affirmation. A few words of kindness could go a long way. "Thank you."

He nodded back at her, something deeper—

but unspoken—lingering in the depths of his gaze. "No. Thank you."

As Serena watched him walk away, she felt something changing inside her.

And she found that fact slightly terrifying.

CHAPTER FIFTEEN

WHEN SERENA CHECKED her social media the next morning, she saw that Khya Smith had already been hard at work. Numerous blogs had been posted, each one calling Serena a boyfriend stealer who'd lured Jeremy to a secluded island where he'd been murdered.

Even though Serena knew she shouldn't do it, she scanned the comment section.

People's remarks were horrible.

Sure, she had a few fans who defended her. But, overall, people had jumped to conclusions and believed what Khya said without doing any research for themselves first.

Serena shouldn't be surprised, but she was disappointed.

How was she going to move past this?

While she contemplated that, Serena's phone rang. It was her Aunt Skye, who also lived here in Lantern Beach. She put the phone to her ear.

"Hey, Skye. What's going on?"

"Listen, it's been awhile since we've chatted. You feel like coming over tonight for dinner with me and Austin?"

"I'd love to." Maybe that was just what she needed to get her mind off everything.

"You can bring Webster too, if you want."

"Webster?"

Skye laughed. "Yeah, you know, your editor and friend?"

"Yes, of course I know who Webster is. But he's probably busy." Was he really busy or was Serena really just panicked that people would think they were together when they weren't?

"If he's not, bring him with you."

"Okay, I'll see you this evening then." That gave Serena something to look forward to. But she had no intention of bringing Webster with her.

She stared at her computer. To post the video or not to post the video? Serena contemplated her options.

If she didn't get ahead of the curve, then Khya would win. Serena couldn't give up just because one person had it in for her.

Instead, she decided to dress like a princess. As always, she would document her transformation and edit the footage for anyone who wanted a tutorial.

Her costume was simple. Nothing fancy about it. It wasn't even that she was dressing like a specific princess.

Serena just wanted to feel like royalty for once in her life.

As she stared at herself in the mirror after she finished getting ready, she thought again about Webster. Thought about the conversation they'd had yesterday.

She'd gotten caught up in the moment.

But now she realized it was a good thing they'd been interrupted. She and Webster would be better off remaining friends. That was all there was to it. She preferred to hold out for one of the former Navy SEALs who lived here on the island, who worked for an organization called Blackout.

Brawn over brains. That was her type.

Serena let out a sigh, feeling surprisingly heavy and burdened today.

Scoops seemed to notice. He jumped into her lap and licked her face.

As a reward, she rubbed the canine's back. "You're always there for me, aren't you?"

She knew what the answer was—a resounding yes. Dog wasn't just a man's best friend. He was a woman's best friend also.

She stood. She wouldn't have time to walk on the beach today. Instead, she needed to get started on her route. In the summer season, there was no time for a break. Breaks were what the winter was for.

AS SERENA STEPPED onto her deck to begin her route, she practically walked right into . . . Webster.

Her hand covered her heart. "Webster. What are you doing here?"

He stared at her, blinking as if surprised, even though he was the one who'd come to find her. "Serena . . . you look . . . beautiful. Like a real-life princess."

Despite herself, she found her cheeks heating. She touched her face, willing it to cool. "Thank you. That's just part of the job, you know."

He pushed his glasses up as he studied her face. "I saw the videos Khya posted about you. I'm sorry."

Serena wasn't sure if it was comforting or not that Webster had followed up online. It had been nice to keep the personal and professional sides of herself separate. But, overall, the notion had been sweet.

"I saw it too," she said. "I'm hoping it will all blow over."

"Let's hope. Otherwise, we need to come up with a plan to fix this smear campaign."

Serena tilted her head. "A plan?"

"We're journalists. We know how to put a spin on things. I'm sure we can figure out a way to help you and to share the truth."

"That's really sweet of you, Webster. Hopefully, it's not going to come down to us doing that. But if it does, I'm definitely all in."

He shifted and played with his glasses again. "Listen, Serena. There's another reason I stopped by so early."

"What's that?" A rumble of nerves rushed through her.

"It's about last night."

"About Kevin being arrested?" Even as she said the words, she knew that wasn't what he was going to talk about.

"No, not about that. About you. About me. About *us*."

Her throat tightened. She should be thrilled that he was bringing up the subject of the two of them, but instead she felt like she couldn't breathe. "Us?"

He stepped closer, emotion pooling in his gaze. "I was hoping that you felt it too."

"Felt something?" Why was she playing dumb? It seemed to be Serena's fallback when she got nervous. She was either loud or she played stupid.

Webster swallowed so hard that his Adam's apple bobbed up and down. "I'm not going to lie, Serena. I like you. I like you a lot, and I have for a while now. I didn't want to say anything out of fear of ruining our friendship. I'm hoping you feel the same way."

Another wave of panic swept through Serena. What did she say? Part of her was intrigued.

But the other part of her . . . wanted to keep things just the way they were.

Because the way they were was safe. Expected.

Friendships were forever.

Boyfriends? They came and went.

Or made it clear they didn't see forever together.

"I don't know, Webster . . ." It pained Serena to say the words, but she couldn't ignore her panic.

He went still. "You don't know . . . how you feel about me?"

Serena rubbed the side of her face, wishing she could disappear from this moment with some kind of princess superpower. "I . . . guess that's what I'm saying. It's all confusing."

Webster frowned but didn't back away. "I know how I feel about you, Serena. And I'm tired of keeping it to myself. So, even if you don't want to pursue anything now, you should know that I'm there waiting for you."

Serena's heart pitter-pattered in her chest. He wasn't pressuring her.

And that only impressed her more—and made her grateful.

"Okay." Her voice sounded hoarse as the word left her throat. "I'll . . . um . . . I'll keep that in mind."

He stepped back, his stiff posture seeming strong and manly.

Or had he always been like that and Serena had just never seen it?

"I've got to turn in my edits this morning and then go interview Ethan about the festival," he said. "We're going to run a follow-up article on it, and I want his thoughts about if this will become an annual event. Maybe we can catch up later?"

"Maybe we can." She nodded a little too quickly.

But as Serena watched Webster walk away, she could hardly breathe.

Whether they remained just friends or if they took their relationship to the next level, she knew that things would never be the same.

CHAPTER SIXTEEN

SERENA COULDN'T STOP THINKING about Webster's proclamation as she worked her normal ice cream route through the island.

She knew it had taken a lot of courage for him to say what he had, that it had been a big risk.

That was impressive. She admired that in a guy. The last thing Serena wanted was a man too afraid to share how he felt. She found bravery very appealing—whether that bravery happened to be emotional or physical.

But Serena and Webster had a good thing going now. Was it worth the risk of ruining that?

Serena didn't know. She was sure that question was going to haunt her for the rest of the day . . . if not longer.

She'd been working for four hours already on this exceedingly hot day. But she was happy to get back into her routine, to entertain little girls with her princess costume, and to let Scoops charm people into buying more ice cream than they'd planned.

Serena turned down another street lined with beach houses and slowed as someone just ahead flagged her down. Overhead, Elsa played "The Ants Go Marching," and outside a stifling heat hung heavy in the August air.

As Serena approached her customer, she leaned out the window and yelled, "World's best ice cream!"

The slogan was a simple but effective hyperbole. She pulled to a stop near the woman waiting on the side of the road with something in her hand.

But Serena's smile disappeared when she realized it was Skippy's mom.

"Look at you." Eloise stepped closer, sweat on her upper lip and her curly hair creating a crown of frizz as it escaped from her ponytail. "You do home deliveries too, huh?"

"This is my main gig," Serena explained. "The festival was just an extra. How has your vacation been going?"

"It's been nice. The beach is beautiful." Eloise's voice sounded unconvinced, however. She looked tired and not at all refreshed. "I figured some ice cream might be a nice reward —for me. I'm going to need a vacation from this vacation, I'm afraid. Isn't it always that way?"

"I hear that a lot." Serena offered a compassionate smile. "You guys heading back soon?"

"We have two more days here." She glanced behind her, as if waiting for Skippy to appear. "My son doesn't do well with change, and he's having a hard time with his father being out to sea."

"I'm sorry to hear that." Serena truly was. She knew about the sacrifices members of the military and their families made. "I hope this week was good for you guys."

Eloise nodded, even though she still looked unconvinced. "It's been fun, but Skippy is a bit of a handful, in case you can't tell."

"Well, you're doing a good job." Serena sensed that the woman needed some encouragement. Didn't everyone? She just seemed so alone, though.

Eloise seemed to snap out of her surprise at Serena's statement and chuckled. "You sell ice cream, and here I am acting like you're a therapist."

"Some people say ice cream can be therapy."

The woman laughed. "Maybe it can. On that note, I'll have a Nutty Buddy."

"One Nutty Buddy coming up." Serena climbed into the back of her truck and grabbed the frozen treat for her. As she handed it to Eloise, conviction solidified inside her. "No charge."

"Oh, don't be silly. Of course I want to pay you." The woman stretched out her hand, offering the five-dollar bill she held.

"This one's on me. Consider it a way of saying thanks for the sacrifices you and your family have made for this country."

Eloise held up her ice cream treat. "Well, thank you. That's very nice of you."

Serena glanced at the house behind the woman, fully expecting to see Skippy appear, asking for a treat. "Speaking of your son, where is he?"

Eloise craned her neck to see over her shoulder. "He was playing in the backyard, but I haven't seen him for a few minutes. That's a good question. He's . . . hard to keep track of sometimes. Too bad I can't have him on a leash."

Just as she said the words, Serena spotted the boy walking behind the neighbor's house.

And in his hands, he was carrying . . . a high-powered bow with a notched arrow.

"SKIPPY, WHERE DID YOU GET THAT?" his mom demanded.

The boy shrugged in defiance. "I'm not going to tell you."

Serena had climbed out of her truck, sensing the woman might need some support right now. Plus . . . there was a bow and arrow.

A bow and arrow.

Her throat tightened as she looked at it.

Skippy didn't want to put it down. But one wrong move, and that arrow could really hurt somebody. It was tucked near the string, just waiting to be flung into the air and hit an unsuspecting target.

Serena knew how bad this situation could turn.

Maybe she should have called Cassidy before talking to Skippy.

His mom wasn't getting through to him. Maybe Serena could think of a way she could help, however.

She bent lower so she could look the boy straight in the eye. "Look, Skippy. How about if I give you a free ice cream sandwich? All you have to do is give me the bow and arrow and tell me where you got it."

His expression remained unchanged. "This is worth more than an ice cream sandwich."

Serena pushed down her irritation at the boy's difficult disposition. "*Two* ice cream sandwiches."

His eyes narrowed even more. "I might be a kid, but I'm not stupid, you know."

Kids definitely weren't her thing. She wasn't sure what she'd been thinking earlier when she'd thought she found her people.

"Okay, what's it going to take for you to tell me where you got that?" Serena had to tap into every ounce of her self-control to keep her words even. She didn't want any high emotions to trigger him. If they did, his finger could slip and . . . Serena didn't want to think about it.

He considered her offer a moment before raising his chin. "I want ten. Ten ice cream sandwiches."

Ten ice cream sandwiches? This boy should be a lawyer one day.

But she was in no mood to argue. The stakes were too high.

"Done." Serena reached for the bow and arrow. "But you're going to have to hand those over to me first."

Skippy hesitated another moment before giving Serena the bow and arrow. As soon as her hands covered the weapon and the arrow was disengaged, relief filled her. At least they were safe.

For now.

"Where did you get these?" Serena asked.

"I need those ice cream sandwiches first."

Serena pushed her irritation aside. Instead, she placed the bow and arrow in her truck, climbed into the back, and grabbed the promised treats. She handed them all to the boy and then waited.

"Well?" she asked.

He unwrapped his first sandwich. "I got them from my neighbor's house."

"Skippy . . ." His mother's voice was laced with disappointment. "You didn't go inside the house, did you? I've talked to you about these things."

"I was just curious. The bow and arrow were sitting in his closet. I figured he doesn't really want them if he's not using them."

Skippy had obviously been coming and going as he pleased. But that was an entirely different issue.

Serena's heart pounded in her ears. "Who lives in that house exactly?"

"The house beside us?" Skippy's mom repeated. "It's Ethan, the director of the children's festival. He must have brought the bow and arrow with him as a prop for one of the stories. Robin Hood maybe?"

Serena tried not to show too much concern on her face. She knew that wasn't the case. This was too much of a coincidence.

And Webster was talking to Ethan right now.

No doubt, they were alone together.

If Ethan even had an inkling that Webster might be onto him . . .

Serena shuddered.

She couldn't waste another moment here.

She had to find Webster and save him . . . especially if she had any hope of finishing their earlier conversation.

CHAPTER SEVENTEEN

AS SERENA HEADED down the road, she called
Cassidy and told her what she'd learned.

The problem was that Webster wasn't
answering his phone—he often turned it off
when he did interviews—and he hadn't made it
clear where this interview with Ethan was taking
place. Cassidy was going to look for him around
town.

"Think, Serena," she muttered to herself as
she gripped the steering wheel. "Think."

She knew Webster well enough that she
should be able to figure out where he might meet
Ethan. There weren't that many places in town to
do interviews. It was too hot to meet outside, and
the newspaper didn't have an official office.

Clearly, Webster hadn't gone to Ethan's rental home. There hadn't been any cars there.

So where might they have met?

Serena could only think of one place that made sense.

The island's municipal offices.

After all, Ethan had worked with island officials to plan this event. Perhaps someone on the tourism board had granted permission to use some space there. The meeting room would be ideal for this kind of thing.

It seemed worth a try.

As Elsa began playing, "Here We Go Looby Loo," Serena pretended like it was a siren and rushed down the road.

A couple of people tried to flag her down to buy some ice cream. Serena smiled and waved at them instead, trying to keep good vibes with potential customers.

She'd come back later.

She hoped.

Serena continued to grip the steering wheel and prayed that all of this would have a happy ending.

A few minutes later, she pulled into the parking lot out front of the city offices. She threw her truck in Park, grabbed Scoops, and ran into the building.

When she stepped inside the lobby, she paused—but only for a minute. The receptionist had placed a "Back in Five" sign on the desk.

With no one to stop her, Serena took off down the hallway. She'd go door to door if she had to, just to make sure that Webster and Ethan weren't here.

But first she headed to the meeting room.

As soon as she got there, she threw the door open.

Webster and Ethan were seated at the table inside.

And Ethan held a . . . sword in the air.

———

"SO NEXT YEAR, we're planning a pirate theme," Ethan said, putting the sword onto the table. "It's going to be some swashbuckling fun. Maybe we can incorporate a pirate-themed dessert." Ethan glanced at Serena for approval.

She barely heard him. Her gaze latched onto Webster.

"Webster, I need you to come with me." Serena sounded breathless as she said the words.

He stood as if startled, and his brow furrowed. "Serena? What are you doing here?"

She glanced at Ethan, trying to confirm he wasn't currently a threat. As he stared at her from the table, she decided she could slow her roll—just a little. The last thing she wanted to do was trigger him.

"Something came up," Serena explained, sucking in another deep breath. "We need to talk. It's important."

"I guess it is." Webster glanced back at Ethan, still in reporter mode. "Do you mind waiting a second?"

Ethan's features looked pinched as he glanced at his watch. "I would, but I'm on a tight time schedule. Maybe we should just wrap this up. I need to get back to my place and pack, so I can catch the next ferry out of here."

Serena couldn't let that happen.

"On second thought, keep doing your interview," she rushed, taking a step back. "I'll wait outside until you're done."

Ethan's gaze narrowed as if he was becoming

suspicious. "No, I think we're good. I'm anxious to get away from here."

"I do have a couple more questions," Webster said.

"Email them to me." Ethan stepped toward the door, as if suddenly in a hurry.

Serena couldn't let him leave. She threw her arm across the doorway, effectively blocking him. "You should stay. Finish the interview in person. Besides, I heard the ferry is already full."

She hadn't actually heard that, but it did happen on occasion. She needed a reason to keep him here until Cassidy could find them.

"Excuse me?" Ethan stared at her, not bothering to hide his annoyance.

Serena needed to think of something else and fast. But her mind went blank.

"Serena, what's going on?" Webster squinted. "Why are you acting so strangely?"

She decided to lay it all on the line. Her gaze locked on Ethan. "Because he killed Jeremy Riser."

Ethan stepped back as horror filled his gaze. "What are you talking about?"

"Don't act clueless. We found your bow and

arrow. The police are on their way to arrest you right now."

The man's face went paler, and his breaths seemed to become shallower. But he said nothing—only stared at her.

"What I can't figure out is why," Serena continued. "Why in the world would you kill somebody who took a picture beside my ice cream truck? I can't think of any connection you and Jeremy might have had."

"It's not like you think it is." Ethan shook his head quickly, frantically.

"So what was it like?" Serena tried to buy time until Cassidy arrived. "Why would you kill an innocent man?"

"I need you to stop talking. And I need to get out of here." Ethan tried to get past her again, but Serena remained in place, planting her feet like trees on the floor.

Webster came to stand beside her. Two against one. Maybe it would work . . . for a while, at least.

Serena heard commotion behind her. Some of the people in the office had to realize something was wrong. She prayed one of them had called the police.

"Why did you do it?" Webster repeated, his body tense as he stared at Ethan.

Sweat scattered across Ethan's skin as he shook his head, his tense body poised for fight or flight. "You don't know what you're talking about."

"You know that we do," Serena said. "I've got the bow and arrow. I'm certain it's going to match the murder weapon. It's just a matter of time before you're arrested. There's no need to deny it any longer."

"I didn't mean to do it, okay!" Ethan wiped his hand over his brow, his motions becoming tighter and tighter.

"Then what happened?" Serena glanced behind her and saw they had an audience in the wings.

One of the men nodded at her, seeming to indicate that help was on the way.

"I was hunting, okay?" Ethan said. "I like to hunt turkeys with a bow. I saw some in those woods near your camper. One walked right across the road as I was driving, and I needed to do something to blow off some steam. I figured, what could it hurt to do a little hunting?"

"How did that end with Jeremy being dead?"

Serena still wanted to understand what had gone down that night.

"I made a bad shot." Ethan rubbed his forehead. "I went to go find my arrow, and there he was. By the time I got to him, he was gone. The arrow went right through his heart."

"So instead of calling for help you dragged him into the woods?" Horror filled Webster's voice.

Serena understood the sentiment. What kind of person did something like that?

"I panicked." Ethan wiped his brow again. As quickly as he did that, more sweat appeared. "I didn't know what to do. By then, it was too late to do anything for him. I had to cover up what I had done. It wasn't my brightest move."

"But it was more than that," Webster said. "Because not only did you kill him and cover it up, you even went above that and managed to cover up all the evidence of what had happened —even the drag marks. The only thing you forgot to do was to clean the blood off the grill of the ice cream truck."

Ethan frowned. "I heard someone coming, and I couldn't finish. I wanted to. Then you came back and moved the truck. I panicked and ran."

"What about Jeremy's hat and wallet?" Serena continued. "Did you plant them at the neighbor's house?"

Ethan's face continued to redden. "His hat and wallet fell from him when I was moving his body. I knew that neighbor of yours was doing drugs—I could smell the pot from your place. I thought . . . maybe if I left those personal items somewhere else, that would distract the police long enough until I could get out of here."

"But you *didn't* leave town." Serena sensed commotion behind her, but she didn't turn to see what was happening. "Why would you stay?"

"If I left in the middle of the festival everyone would be suspicious. That's why I was planning on leaving as soon as I finished this interview." His gaze went to the sword, as if he contemplated grabbing it. "I've worked so hard to develop my brand, my career. Why couldn't you just leave well enough alone? I was this close to getting away with it."

Just then, Cassidy charged between Serena and Webster. "Ethan Murphy, you're under arrest."

She'd obviously heard everything that Ethan had just said.

"I promise, I didn't mean to. I didn't mean to!" Panic captured Ethan's voice as Cassidy slapped some handcuffs on him.

It looked like justice really had been served.

Ethan truly had been a fixer—he'd just been on the other end of trouble this time. His mistake wouldn't allow his public persona to survive. So he'd tried to hide that part of his life.

"Good job, you two." Cassidy paused beside Serena and Webster as an officer led Ethan away. "I'm going to need you to give me the murder weapon and come down to the station and give your statements."

"Of course," Serena said. "No problem."

She was just glad this was all over.

CHAPTER EIGHTEEN

A FEW HOURS LATER, Serena and Webster were cleared to leave the police station.

As they stepped outside, they turned to each other. Serena felt a rush of nerves rake through her as she stared at Webster. She couldn't get their earlier conversation out of her mind.

Should they talk about it now?

Before she could say anything, Webster pulled her into his embrace. "It was awfully brave what you did back there, Serena."

"I don't know about brave," she muttered into his chest. "Maybe stupid. I just didn't want Ethan to leave the island without having justice served —and I was afraid he might turn on you if he thought you were onto him."

"Thankfully, that didn't happen."

Serena stepped back. "What do you think is next for him?"

"If Jeremy's death had just been accidental, Ethan would have been a lot better off. But when he tried to cover things up, that's when Ethan's trouble really started for him."

"I agree. He just made a bad situation worse."

Serena looked behind her as she sensed someone walking toward them.

Khya Smith stood there, her eyes red with tears. Instead of walking into the police station where she'd been headed, she paused beside them.

"Thanks for figuring out what happened to Jeremy," she started, reluctance lingering in her voice. "I'm sorry I was so angry with you, I Am Quick Change. But you were the only person who made sense as the guilty party, and I needed someone to blame."

"It's okay." Serena didn't want to say the words. She wanted to be angry. But the woman had already been through a lot, and anger wouldn't help the situation. Maybe grace would.

"I found Jeremy's planner. He made some notes there under the "Goals" section. It turns out, he was interested in creating a website for you. He thought the exposure would help him build his brand. He really thought you had something good going, and he wanted to get in on the ground floor of it."

"So no secret crushes, huh?" Serena said, doing her best not to sound smug.

Khya shook her head. "No, I don't think so. I'll run a retraction. I'll admit that you and Jeremy weren't together, and that I was wrong. I hope I can undo some of the damage I did. I'm . . . sorry."

With that, the woman slipped inside the police station.

That had been easier than Serena had ever imagined it might be.

She didn't need a fixer in her life after all.

Just as Khya disappeared inside, someone else walked out: Skippy and Eloise.

For the first time since Serena had seen him, the boy actually looked remorseful.

The two stopped in front of Serena and Webster.

"What do you need to say?" Eloise asked Skippy.

"I'm sorry." Skippy pulled his gaze up, his

red-rimmed eyes meeting Serena's. "I'm going to do better."

"I hope you do," Serena said. "You can't break into people's homes and steal things."

"Chief Chambers was able to get up with Skippy's father on the phone," Eloise explained. "He and his dad had a really long talk, and I think Skippy now understands the gravity of the situation."

"That's good news," Webster said.

"Frank—that's my husband—will be getting out of the military in a few more months, so I think that will make a world of difference."

"Plus, I have to clean up trash around town." Skippy frowned.

"Chief Chambers said he needs to spend today doing that here—it was that or being locked up."

"Sounds like you made the right choice." Serena nodded at the boy.

"And he's been grounded from Fortnite until he gets his act together."

The boy's frown grew deeper, but he didn't argue.

"We need to get busy," Eloise said. "But it was

nice to meet you both. Thank you so much for being gracious to us."

As they said goodbye, Serena couldn't help but reflect on how good had come out of a bad situation. What Skippy had done was wrong, but it had led them to finding the killer.

"So what now?" Serena asked Webster when it was just the two of them.

He frowned. "It looks like I have an article to write."

"I guess you do." She glanced at the time on her phone. "Speaking of which, I promised Skye and Austin I would eat dinner with them. You want to come? I'm sure they'd love to have you."

A sad smile tugged at his lips. "I would. But I really do need to start this article. I've had too much fun this week selling banana splits instead of working."

"Speaking of which, you do look a little exhausted." Small circles stretched beneath his eyes.

He shrugged. "Maybe a rain check for a different time."

"That sounds good."

But if Serena didn't like Webster, why did her

heart ache just a little as she walked away from him now?

IT HAD BEEN nice catching up with Skye and Austin over some homemade shrimp scampi—made with shrimp fresh from the Pamlico Sound.

Serena tried to keep her aunt and uncle entertained with stories about what had happened this week and all her various ice cream adventures. She'd always been told she was a natural-born storyteller and entertainer. She certainly had a lot of fodder after this summer.

But as the three of them settled down with some hot chocolate in front of the outdoor fire pit, Serena could feel a shift coming in the conversation.

When Austin slipped back inside to take a phone call, Skye turned to her. "So, I've been meaning to ask . . . what's going on between you and Webster?"

Serena's eyes widened at the question. "Me and Webster?"

Skye gave her a look. "Come on. You're not fooling me. I've known you since you were in diapers."

Serena shrugged. "We're friends."

"You seem like more than that—you're attached at the hip lately. And both of your faces light up when you're around each other."

Was that really true? Serena had never noticed before—or thought about it. "It's complicated."

"You know, Austin and I started off as best friends." Skye stared at the fire as her fingers gripped the hand-thrown mug in her hands.

"I remember it clearly. I thought neither one of you would ever really admit your feelings for each other." How could they have been so blind? It was clear to everyone around them that the two were meant to be together.

Were people saying that about her and Webster?

"And now I'm so glad that we did take that risk and share our feelings," Skye said. "I've never been happier."

Serena let out a breath as she considered what she would say next. "Webster's a good guy. He really is. It's just that he's so . . . square."

"Sometimes what you think you want, isn't what you want at all, and it's definitely not what you need."

"I suppose." But Serena needed to think on that another moment.

"Does Webster make you a better person?"

Serena thought about all the two of them had been through together over the summer. "He's been there for me throughout everything. I guess he does help balance me out. He is more logical than I am, and that's been a big help. But we're also alike in a lot of ways. We both love scouting out the truth and finding answers."

"Then maybe you do want to give it a try." Skye shrugged as the orange glow of the fire warmed her face. "You'll never know how great you might be together unless you make that leap."

"I don't want to get hurt either." Maybe that was the truth of the matter. Sometimes Serena wondered if she was even girlfriend material—or if she was simply destined to be everyone's best friend. She had a lot of weirdness that a person would need to accept.

But at this point, Webster should realize good and well just how weird she was.

"Nobody wants to get hurt, Serena," Skye said. "But that's the risk that you have to take if you want to discover something that could be great. Not only when it comes to love, but when it comes to life in general."

Her aunt's words washed over her. Serena had been hiding behind all her different personalities for a long time now. Too long. It was easier to pretend to be someone else sometimes than it was to show people who you really were.

But what kind of way to live was that? Ethan had been all about image and look where that had gotten him—probably he'd be sent to prison.

"You know what?" Serena muttered. "You're right. Life does require risk."

"It does."

Serena handed her mug back to Skye and popped to her feet. "You've given me clarity. I'm going to go talk to Webster now. I don't want to wait any longer."

"You do that."

Serena grabbed Scoops and escaped to her ice cream truck.

She was about to take one of the biggest risks

of her life—something far bigger than a new ice cream flavor or changing up her daily route.

She was about to take a risk on . . . love.

CHAPTER NINETEEN

SERENA KNOCKED ON ERNESTINE SANDERS' door and waited—albeit impatiently. She had to force herself not to keep knocking until someone answered.

Ernestine was Webster's aunt, and Webster was currently staying at her place.

A few minutes later, Ernestine opened the door. She pulled her house robe tighter around her waist, a confused expression across her face.

"Serena? Is everything okay?" Ernestine glanced behind Serena, as if looking for trouble.

"I need to talk to Webster. Is he here?"

She let out a breath. "I thought kids these days just used their phones."

"Usually. But there's something I really need to discuss with him face-to-face. It can't wait."

Earnestine let out an unamused laugh. "And here I thought there was a fire. Anyway, I'm sorry to say it, but he's not here."

Serena's heart sank as all the bravado that had built up inside her seemed to deflate. "Do you know where he is?"

"He didn't tell me. I'm sorry. I wish I could help."

Serena glanced at her watch. It was already eleven. Where could Webster be at this hour?

She tried to ignore the disappointment filling her, but she couldn't. The need to talk to Webster pressed on her until she couldn't ignore it. She'd never been so sure of anything before.

"Thank you," Serena muttered to Ernestine as she hurried back to her ice cream truck.

So much for declaring her love for him.

Maybe this was a sign.

As Serena climbed back into Elsa and took off down the road, Serena realized she couldn't go back to her camper and sit alone with her thoughts. She'd drive herself crazy if she did.

Instead, she pulled into a public parking lot

near the beach. Putting Scoops on a leash, the two of them walked toward the ocean.

The water always helped to soothe her when her heart felt disheveled. Maybe the cadence of the crashing waves would work its magic tonight also.

The beachfront was dark tonight. Really dark. Lantern Beach didn't have streetlights, which made for some amazing views of the stars. Tonight, the heavens were putting on their show. In fact, the Milky Way stretched above her now.

Serena paused and stared up at it for a minute. "Isn't it beautiful, Scoops?"

The dog happily trotted beside her, his tongue wagging.

Serena had a good life here on the island. A really good life. In fact, there wasn't much she would change. Even through all the struggles for money and the storms that the island had experienced, she wouldn't trade the place for the world.

She continued walking, trying to work out her thoughts.

As she got closer to the area where the beach art was left, she spotted a shadow on the shoreline.

She paused and sucked in a breath.

It was the creator of the beach art, wasn't it?

He—or she—was here.

Creating a new masterpiece.

It was time Serena figured out exactly who was behind those creations.

IT WAS TOO dark to make out any of the person's features—everything was shadowed. Instead, Serena pulled out her phone.

She'd take a picture instead.

She hit the button, and a flash lit the beach.

The artist yelped and staggered backward, shielding his face from the blinding light.

Serena had surprised him as much as he'd surprised her.

But, as quickly as the illumination had materialized, it disappeared.

Serena glanced at her screen, trying to make out the image of the person.

She couldn't wait to see who was behind this.

"What do you think you're doing?" someone grumbled.

She recognized that voice. Was it . . . ?

Serena glanced at the picture again, and her eyes widened.

"Webster?"

"Serena?"

She looked up and saw Webster standing in front of her. Buckets of shells scattered around the space, serving as nature's paint palate for his creations. Sand covered his hands and knees.

He was definitely creating something.

"You've been behind this?" Maybe Serena should have seen it earlier. The beachside designs hadn't started appearing until Webster had come to town. But she'd never seen him as the artistic type. He was too straitlaced.

"I've always done art on the side," Webster admitted with a shrug. "My parents didn't encourage it. They wanted me to get a real career."

Serena continued to stare at him, her thoughts clashing as she processed this new development. "I had no idea you were the one behind these. They're gorgeous."

He smiled. "Thank you. It gives me something to do when I can't sleep at night."

"You're an insomniac?" No wonder he looked so tired all the time.

"I am. I'm lucky to get a few hours of sleep at night. But I've learned to adjust and use my creative energy in different ways."

Serena stepped closer, something cracking in her heart. "Webster . . ."

"What are you doing out here, Serena?" His voice softened, almost sounding tender.

"I went to find you, but your aunt said you weren't home. I had no idea you'd be here."

He raised his hands and shrugged. "Here I am."

"Webster . . ." Her voice caught.

"Yes?"

What did Serena want to say exactly? She licked her lips, desperately needing to say the right thing. "You continue to surprise me."

"Surprises can be good, right?"

She nodded. "Yes, they can. What's even more surprising is the fact that you appeared in my life. You're not the person I expected. But you're just the person I needed. You're the person that I thought I'd never find . . ."

He stepped closer—or was that gravity that seemed to pull them together?

Either way, Serena wasn't complaining.

"Is that right?" Webster murmured.

"The truth is, my breakup back in Michigan wasn't as easy as I made it sound. When I told my boyfriend I was moving, he said it was just as well because he'd never seen a future with me. He said I was the kind of girl guys loved having as a friend but not a wife."

"Ouch."

"I felt more rejected than I thought I would. Afterward, I found it easier just to have crushes on unreachable guys than I did to truly look at guys whom I might care about. But I'm tired of living like that."

Serena swallowed hard as she waited for Webster's response. Would he think she was crazy? Would this be the moment when he saw who she really was and decided she was too much for him? That she was indeed better off remaining a friend?

She could hardly breathe as he stared at her.

Finally, Webster said, "Those words are music to my ears, Serena."

He moved closer and brushed a hair out of her eyes. As he gazed at her, warmth filled Serena like a fireplace on a cold day—warmth that she never wanted to stop experiencing.

Without any more hesitation, Serena leaned

forward. Her lips met Webster's. The feelings inside her seemed to whisk her away like driftwood caught in the ocean's tide.

She could really get used to this.

Scoops barked beside them and bounced up in between them with a fury.

The two of them stepped back and chuckled.

The next instant, Scoops jumped into Serena's arms. As the three of them stood on the beach together, Serena had a good feeling that they were going to be a team for a long, long time.

In fact, she had visions of Elsa traveling down the road with strings of cans rattling against the asphalt and "Just Married" painted on her back windows.

What song might Elsa be playing?

That was easy. "Going to the Chapel."

But, for now, Serena was going to help Webster finish his beach art—which just happened to be a heart.

COMPLETE BOOK LIST

#12 Cunning Attractions

#13 Cold Case: Clean Getaway

#14 Cold Case: Clean Sweep

#15 Cold Case: Clean Break

#16 Cleans to an End (coming soon)

While You Were Sweeping, A Riley Thomas Spinoff

The Sierra Files:

#1 Pounced

#2 Hunted

#3 Pranced

#4 Rattled

The Gabby St. Claire Diaries (a Tween Mystery series):

The Curtain Call Caper

The Disappearing Dog Dilemma

The Bungled Bike Burglaries

The Worst Detective Ever

#1 Ready to Fumble

#2 Reign of Error

#3 Safety in Blunders

#4 Join the Flub

#5 Blooper Freak

#6 Flaw Abiding Citizen

#7 Gaffe Out Loud

#8 Joke and Dagger

#9 Wreck the Halls

#10 Glitch and Famous (coming soon)

Raven Remington

Relentless 1

Relentless 2 (coming soon)

Holly Anna Paladin Mysteries:

#1 Random Acts of Murder

#2 Random Acts of Deceit

#2.5 Random Acts of Scrooge

#3 Random Acts of Malice

#4 Random Acts of Greed

#5 Random Acts of Fraud

#6 Random Acts of Outrage

#7 Random Acts of Iniquity

Lantern Beach Mysteries

#1 Hidden Currents

#2 Flood Watch

#3 Storm Surge

#4 Dangerous Waters

#5 Perilous Riptide

Deadman's Float

Milkshake Up

Bomb Pop Threat (coming soon)

Banana Split Personalities (coming soon)

The Sidekick's Survival Guide

The Art of Eavesdropping

The Perks of Meddling

The Exercise of Interfering

The Practice of Prying (coming soon)

Carolina Moon Series

Home Before Dark

Gone By Dark

Wait Until Dark

Light the Dark

Taken By Dark

Suburban Sleuth Mysteries:

Death of the Couch Potato's Wife

Fog Lake Suspense:

Edge of Peril

Margin of Error

Brink of Danger

Line of Duty

Cape Thomas Series:

Dubiosity

Disillusioned

Distorted

Standalone Romantic Mystery:

The Good Girl

Suspense:

Imperfect

The Wrecking

Sweet Christmas Novella:

Home to Chestnut Grove

Standalone Romantic-Suspense:

Keeping Guard

The Last Target

Race Against Time

Ricochet

Key Witness

Lifeline

High-Stakes Holiday Reunion

Desperate Measures

Hidden Agenda

Mountain Hideaway

Dark Harbor

Shadow of Suspicion

The Baby Assignment

The Cradle Conspiracy

Trained to Defend

Nonfiction:

Characters in the Kitchen

Changed: True Stories of Finding God through Christian Music (out of print)

The Novel in Me: The Beginner's Guide to Writing and Publishing a Novel (out of print)

ABOUT THE AUTHOR

USA Today has called Christy Barritt's books "scary, funny, passionate, and quirky."

Christy writes both mystery and romantic suspense novels that are clean with underlying messages of faith. Her books have won the Daphne du Maurier Award for Excellence in Suspense and Mystery, have been twice nominated for the Romantic Times Reviewers' Choice Award, and have finaled for both a Carol Award and Foreword Magazine's Book of the Year.

She is married to her Prince Charming, a man who thinks she's hilarious—but only when she's not trying to be. Christy is a self-proclaimed klutz, an avid music lover who's known for spontaneously bursting into song, and a road trip aficionado.

When she's not working or spending time with her family, she enjoys singing, playing the guitar, and exploring small, unsuspecting towns where people have no idea how accident-prone she is.

Find Christy online at:
www.christybarritt.com
www.facebook.com/christybarritt
www.twitter.com/cbarritt

Sign up for Christy's newsletter to get information on all of her latest releases here: www.christybarritt.com/newsletter-sign-up/

If you enjoyed this book, please consider leaving a review.